W9-BPS-416

The Last
NEWSPAPER
MN

A novel by
Mark Di Ionno

Plexus Publishing, Inc.
Medford, New Jersey

First printing, 2012

The Last Newspaperman

Copyright © 2012 by Mark Di Ionno

Published by:
Plexus Publishing Inc.
143 Old Marlton Pike
Medford, NJ 08055

Library of Congress Cataloging-in-Publication Data

Di Ionno, Mark.
  The last newspaperman : a novel / by Mark Di Ionno.
    p. cm.
  ISBN 978-0-937548-74-5
  1. Reporters and reporting--Fiction. I. Title.
  PS3604.I114L37 2012
  813'.6--dc23

                                                                2012014373

ISBN 978-0-937548-74-5

Printed and bound in the United States of America.

President and CEO: Thomas H. Hogan, Sr.
Editor-in-Chief and Publisher: John B. Bryans
VP Graphics and Production: M. Heide Dengler
Managing Editor: Amy M. Reeve
Editorial Assistant: Brandi Scardilli
Book Designer: Kara M. Jalkowski
Cover Designer: Denise M. Erickson
Copyeditor: Beverly Michaels
Proofreader: Sheryl McGrotty
Marketing Coordinator: Rob Colding

www.plexuspublishing.com

For my mentor, Jerry Izenberg, The Last Sportswriter

Prologue

L et me tell you a little story.

In sixth grade, I had a sweet, frail nun named Sister Lucia, who taught religion by telling stories about ancient saints and the torture they endured from pagan Christian-haters. She spoke with an airy Italian accent, and her narratives sounded like delicate fingers running randomly over high notes on a piano. "Let me tell-a you a *BEEuTEEful* story," she would say.

She was a kind old lady with genuine affection for children and, unlike most of the older nuns, refrained from jabbing or slapping us. She disciplined instead by withdrawing. A bad kid could turn Sister Lucia distant and businesslike, and, for the many of us who loved her, that stung more than any ruler slap on the knuckles.

She was short and bony, and had a swiveling limp that made her body sway to such degrees that she walked like a penguin.

The summer before sixth grade, before I ever heard Sister Lucia's "beautiful stories," I began filling the overcast days and the lightning bug-lit evenings by keeping a journal. Not a very boyish thing to do, but I did, nonetheless.

At the local 5 & 10, I bought a half-dozen pearly essay books, the kind we used in school. Three were black-covered and three light blue. I wrote my name and address on the inside covers as soon as I got home. My plan for these books was not girly, like unloading my feelings or rehashing school gossip. My plan was to record little snippets of stories about adults I knew. Adults fascinated me, for reasons I didn't understand at the time.

The black books were for family members. The blue books were for everybody else: teachers and nuns; parents of friends; the mailman, Mr. Smythe; Willie, the produce clerk at the market; Dom

DiGuiseppe, the landscaper who maintained our yard with a crew who understood only Spanish unless Dom was talking.

I collected these story bits the way other kids collected baseball cards or butterflies: partly to learn, partly to have something that was just mine. Something to hold onto. For two years I wrote, and I still have the books—all six lashed together by extra-large rubber bands—kept safe in a fireproof filing cabinet where I store my important papers. I look at them now and then, reading over my labored Palmer method script, now a faded No. 2-lead gray, and remember the people: how they talked, where they talked, what the weather was when they talked. The journal entries can be like photographs that way.

Mostly, though, I remember writing. Holding the pencil so tight my fingers would become indented and turn pale. Racing to write before I forgot what people told me. Most of the entries are written in the voices of the subjects—or, at least, my version of their voices—and in this way, they are like tape recordings. In this, I am gifted. I can record details accurately because I can hear the storyteller's voice in my head.

Looking back, I collected stories because I had so few of my own—and the most telling were locked away in early childhood subconscious, a place I cannot get to.

The stories I can reach begin at age five or so, when I went to live with my Aunt Mag and Uncle Dave. They are normal stories about a safe childhood on a suburban cul-de-sac, with friendly neighbors and nice kids.

Aunt Mag and Uncle Dave had no children. They were older than my parents, but not by as much as it seemed. They belonged to a country club and played golf. They had cocktail parties. My Aunt Mag was, and is, a good-looking woman; not the homey, doting aunt type. I always felt excited shame when I saw her in underwear, which was often, because on many nights after my bedtime, she got ready to "go out" with Uncle Dave. My room was across the hall from theirs, and from my dark bed I saw her back and front as she flipped and teased her silvery blonde hair while seated in front of her vanity mirror in a bra and panties. She would then slip on a black cocktail dress or silky print thing, and come in and kiss me good night (while I pretended to sleep), before leaving me with my grandmother or whatever neighborhood teenage girl was available.

Uncle Dave was trim and wore shiny suits to work, and he had a vintage convertible T-Bird, polished and chromed to the nines.

My aunt and uncle were more manicured grown-ups than my mother was, at least the way I remember it. They made a nice room for me and furnished it with department store boy stuff. Sports and space motif sheets and comforters, a football piggy bank, a few airplane and car models (including a T-Bird just like Uncle Dave's, down to the maroon body and black top), a bat and ball desk lamp.

Aunt Mag was my mother's sister, older by five years, but was much more stylish and worldly. My mother, I guess, never had a chance to grow accustomed to those things.

My mother was pretty and slender like Aunt Mag, but in a plain, more girlish way. And darker, with hair that was almost black.

I remember her young—dark hair pulled back tight, smoking a cigarette and wearing sunglasses—as I splashed in a plastic pool in the backyard of a house I don't remember. She would be very still for long moments, until I wondered if she were asleep. Then she would slowly raise the cigarette to her lips. I see her swinging on the front porch of another house—my grand-mother's?—the *squeak-squaw* of the chains lulling me to sleep on the sheet-covered living room couch just inside the screen door, watching a swirl of cigarette smoke gather around her head like ocean fog on those dead-air summer nights.

I remember her hugging me so tight it scared me to tears, and I couldn't tell if the wetness on our faces and deep heaves in our chests were mine or hers or both.

I have little recollection of my father, but I have a few pictures. My dad, handsome and broad-shouldered with a side-of-the-mouth smile and dark hair slicked back, holding me bundled in baby blankets; me, at eight or nine months, chuckling in a sluggers suit—him, in a T-shirt, squatting down and propping me up with one hand while he points at the camera with the other; me riding high on his shoulders with my hands grabbing fistfuls of hair like horse reins, even though he holds me firmly with both hands. The pictures were taken in front of the house I don't remember, all in bright sunlight. In every picture, my dad is squinting or wearing sunglasses, but now, more than ever, I can see I am his son. I'm older now than my dad was in those pictures, and in the mirror, I see what he might have looked like approaching middle age: same large slim nose, crooked smile, thin face, and pointy jaw grown somewhat fleshy. In every picture, I just came to realize, he is holding me up.

With those pictures, I also keep a newspaper clipping. Its headline reads WEST BELMAR DAD KILLED IN CRASH.

It's a straightforward account of how my father lost control of his Pontiac Grand Prix one rainy night on a nasty curve on Route 35 in Belmar, New Jersey, just beyond the drawbridge over the Shark River Inlet. He hadn't been drinking but wasn't wearing a seatbelt, according to the investigating officer, Sgt. Harry Conklin. Speed may have been a factor, he said. The article then had neighbors talking about the multitude of horrific crashes on the curve and how the state should put up flashing lights or guard rails. The article said my dad, 31, was a communications worker at Fort Monmouth and was survived by a wife, and a son. Me.

It did not say if he was a faithful husband or an attentive father, or a man with a history or dreams. He was, in short, a daily tragedy, as one-dimensional as the paper the news of his death was printed on. Here today, gone tomorrow; never revisited by anyone but those affected directly, especially my mother.

Mercifully, my dad died in the days before the internet. These days, the electronic versions of such stories on news websites invite anonymous reader comments, and they are typically uninformed and often cruel. I read these types of stories now and the comments that follow, and I get depressed, for this is what we do with the noble ideal of Free Speech:

> *What kind of freakin' idiot doesn't wear a seatbelt? He*
> *deserved to die.*
> *Not drinking? Right. Must have some cop buddies.*
> *Just what we need, more lights and guard rails, paid for*
> *by taxpayers, to protect a freakin' fool that speeds.*

Graffiti on grief. The cowardice of anonymity. We've become a society that piles on without much regard for how tragedy and loss shape the lives of those left behind. Glimpses of cataclysmic events—genocide, war and terror, fire, earthquakes and floods, murder on our streets—come into our lives and then go.

We never follow these people to see how they absorb, then endure, the impact of their loss or pain or humiliation. Once the story is over or the show is done, they have served their purpose: to entertain us, however briefly. Their public stint is up; they go back to salvage their privacy. As a former newspaperman, I'm embarrassed ever to have taken part.

I keep the pictures of my parents and the news clipping of my father's accident inside the cover of my first journal, along with the Mass card from my mother's funeral. My father's death was public; hers was just as lonely, but private.

She was never the same after the accident. Aunt Mag says she "got sick." She teetered, then fell, then was crushed by the weight of being left alone with a child about to embark on a boyhood his dad wouldn't be there to share. Cub Scouts, Little League, fishing. All things part of a life she dreamed of and counted on, but lost after a skidless crash on a wet road on a dangerous curve on an otherwise ordinary night. The randomness of such bad luck, I think, is enough to make anybody "sick." Anxiety and depression followed, chased by tranquilizers and antidepressants. One drug led to another, and she never got "well."

I was sent to Aunt Mag's, and I remember a few times my mother came to take me home. I could hear her muffled voice downstairs as she talked to Aunt Mag. I would hear Aunt Mag say in a stern whisper, "No, kid, not yet. Look at you. You're not ready." And then the screen door would creak and slam, and the tires of her car would kick up gravel, pebbles dinging off metal, each distinct and alone in their sound.

She came and went that way throughout my childhood. For years, I would lie in the dark, surrounded by my little boy things, and close my eyes tight and try hard to remember anything else about my parents. My father's hands. His effortless lifts. The scent of my mother. Her smile. Her kiss.

Nothing.

Every night I would search the darkness in my head, hoping some vision would appear under my eyelids; something clear, like those sunny pictures I had, with their runny Kodak colors. Something mine. Something I could touch and bring back anytime I wanted.

But it never happened. No matter how hard I tried, my early childhood remained blackly opaque.

With so many blanks impossible to fill, I grew curious about people in my life and asked them to fill in blanks for me.

I asked Uncle Dave what he was like as a teen, and he told me about his first car, a metallic blue Ford Falcon, souped up to run with the Barracudas, Mustangs, and Road Runners of the day. Aunt Mag told me about when she and Mom were little, and how my grandfather took them fishing for sunnies on the small, freshwater intercoastal lakes we lived near at the Jersey Shore. My grandmother talked about my grandfather, long gone, and his love for fishing, despite his daughters' girly squeals, and his eccentric taste for eels, which she said "was like frying a big slimy worm." She told me how he "caught lung cancer," smoking two packs of Luckies a day, and warned me off cigarettes.

Mr. Smythe told me about Korea and how veterans got Civil Service points on the Postal Exam so he became a mailman. Walking was tough, though, and he still spit out shrapnel "made in China" now and then. Dom DiGuiseppe told me how he started his business when he was not more than my age, building a half-million-dollar-a-year landscaping enterprise from nothing more than his grandfather's push mower, a wagon he would pack with bags of grass clippings, a "willingness to sweat and the discipline to save." Willie, the produce guy, told me how he learned about fruit and vegetables on his family farm in Allaire, which went belly up and was now covered by "executive estates." He explained how to tell the difference between a Jersey tomato and "those hothouse jobs" from California. "The Jerseys are blotchy and misshapen and uglier, but much more flavorful," he said. "Just like our people."

That's what my journal entries were. The adult answers to a kid's questions. The beginnings of bigger stories.

***

In school, I became friendly enough with Sister Lucia to one day ask her why she limped.

I did this without fear. She was especially tender with me because she knew my family, and she approached me with sympathy and care.

I asked innocently enough, expecting to hear she had been hit by a car or had fallen off a horse as a child. Or maybe something less traumatic: a birth defect, like a curved spine or uneven legs.

"Sister Lucia? Why do you limp?"

She turned to me with a series of expressions I can still replay in my mind. I never knew a face could move so fast. The first curtain was stunned pain; someone stung by a bee. The next was a flash of anger at that pain. Her eyes narrowed, their cataract cloudiness now clear; an assassin looking through crosshairs. Her pasty, wrinkled skin filled with blood, making her suddenly look healthier and younger, and capable of inflicting serious corporal punishment on me.

Then, in a rapid eye-blink before pulling the trigger, she saw me for me; not an insolent wiseass, but a curious little boy in a wrinkled white shirt and blue school clip-on tie, with matching blue pants hitched sloppy at the waist and smudged with powdery chalk dust. A vulnerable boy, deserving of her gentle sympathy, now terrified by her anger.

A boy who, maybe like her, was a random victim of bad circumstance.

She limped; I had dark holes I could not fill.

We both knew that about one another.

Only she knew the "why" for us both.

My question, she must have thought in those moments, was a fair one, one designed to level the playing field, an awkward attempt at bonding.

Her face softened.

The kindness returned, but then something else changed in her face. There was some wrestling in her mind, a flash of indecision, followed by a look of resignation. She made a deep sigh, a prelude to the unpleasant task of confession.

Then she patted the chair beside her.

"Sit down," she said. "Let me tell you a little story. But you must promise to keep it a secret ..."

I swore to God, sat, and listened.

"When I was a little girl, my real name was Catalina Cataldi, and I lived with my family in a village on the outskirts of Sira'Cusa, a town in Sicily. The patron saint of that town is-a Saint Lucia, whose name I took when I came out of the convent in Catania. This is why you call me Sister Lucia. That was a long, long time ago, in the 1910s. I was just 16, not much older than the eighth grade girls here.

"I took that name because ... well, let me tell you."

The story went like this:

Saint Lucia was born in Roman times—times when Christians were persecuted and tortured and fed to the lions. Her father was a wealthy Roman, a pagan. He died when Saint Lucia was a girl, 15 maybe. Her mother, also a pagan without faith, was so afraid of being poor she tried to sell her beautiful young daughter off in marriage to an older man, another pagan who had been friends with Lucia's father. Now, somewhere along the way in this pagan village, little Lucia gained piety and wanted to love only Christ, so she would not submit to the marriage. She rejected the man, and he grew violent and angry. He beat her and called the Roman guards to take her to prison. When they came to get her, her feet were mysteriously fixed to the ground. The soldiers could not budge her. So they brought down a team of oxen to drag her away and hitched her to the beasts with leather straps. The guards beat those poor animals until their hides tore, but even they could not budge Lucia. The townspeople gathered and fell to their knees when they realized they were witnessing a miracle; the power of Lucia's faith gave her the strength to fend off the Roman guards. The frustrated soldiers then unhitched the exhausted oxen and built a bonfire around Lucia. But each time they tried to light it, the wood miraculously began to sweat, extinguishing the flames. When the guards finally gave up and her ordeal was over, Lucia simply walked away, through the crowd of praying villagers. Some reached to touch her clothing; most dared not look.

But Lucia's work on earth was not done. She converted all the people of her village and the surrounding towns where her legend grew, then finally, all of Sicily. But the Romans did not forget. One night many months later they came for Lucia. God whispered to her, "Now, Lucia, your work is done, and your reward waits in heaven." He allowed her to be martyred.

"I won't tell you these details because they are so gruesome," Sister Lucia said. "But she experienced no pain, only joy to be in God's grace. But that was her story.

"Now mine …

"Like Lucia, I was a beautiful young girl, believe it or not, some said the most pretty in my village. My parents were poor farmers, who worked on the land of a big, ugly man named Giancarlo Graceffa. My mother did not like the way he looked at me as I cut hay in the field and told me, 'Never be alone with that man.'

"But, as time went on, Giancarlo did little things to favor my parents: a few more lire for their bushels here, extra time with the plough horse there, a few more jugs from the well. My mother softened her position. One day, Giancarlo and his wife were in a wagon crash. The wagon slid off the dirt road on their hill and flipped over. Giancarlo managed to jump but his poor wife was crushed. A few weeks later, Giancarlo came to our house and offered my parents clear title to the land they farmed and 100,000 lire for my hand in marriage. My parents gave permission, but I did not. A wedding was arranged with the mayor, not the priest, and I was dragged to the village square. I said, 'no, never,' during the vows, but the mayor said we were married anyway. There was a reception where the men got drunk and the women wept. Remember, I said reception, not celebration, because it was not happy. The men drank to forget their anger at Giancarlo, and the women cried in sadness and sympathy for me.

"After the wedding I refused to go home with Giancarlo. My father, who was drunk and embarrassed by my defiance, slapped me twice, then threw me over his shoulder and carried me up the hill. I kicked, pulled his hair, and punched his head the whole way up, bloodying his lip and bruising my knuckles. He threw me into Giancarlo's arms and said, 'She's your problem now,' wiping the blood from his mouth."

Sister Lucia looked out the window, her eyes becoming clouded and distant. She was back there, in the story. I was all but forgotten. I remained quiet and followed her gaze out to the grotto in front of the church, which held a replica of Michelangelo's mournful *The Pieta*. Around it were the fresh, yellow daffodils of spring. Behind it, the flag pole where the American flag rose and fell in the wind.

"Giancarlo moved to me but I told him I had, well, a lady's illness, and he should leave me alone for a few days. He showed me to a room and let me alone for the night, and the next night, too. But I knew this could only last so long. I had to escape. On the third night, I packed up my few things and crept down the stairs to run away, but found Giancarlo snoring in a straw chair propped against the door. I tiptoed to the back door, but there I found his old lady housemaid, Matilda, asleep in a chair against the door, her eyes fluttering in dream. On the counter was a small meat cleaver, which I decided to take for my protection in the dark night.

"I went back up to my room and quietly tried to climb over the rail of the balcony to lower myself down. But my skirt got caught, and I fell off the rail and landed badly. My leg was jammed up into my hip, and the socket chipped, and my leg bone cracked. I began to run, even with the terrible pain. I prayed to God to help me escape. Just then I heard Giancarlo yell from the front door, calling me names I would not repeat. And then I heard the blast from his shotgun. Ba-BOOM! I kept running and praying, but the pain was crippling me, and I stumbled and fell. I heard Giancarlo's footsteps and his heavy breath on my neck, then his paws on my back. He was sweaty and also stunk from cigars and wine. He pushed me flat on the ground face down and held my wrists. I could hardly breathe. With no breath, I couldn't inhale to scream. He picked me up to drag me to his house, but I started to flail at him. I can't remember if I had the cleaver in my hand or not. I gasped for air, and a strange hot, desert wind rushed into my lungs. An ethereal power filled me. I knew immediately it was something sacred.

"'*Gesu, Cristo, Aiutami!*' I screamed. 'Jesus Christ, please help me!' My scream knocked Giancarlo back like he was kicked by a horse. He looked stunned and stumbled back, then went bug-eyed and clutched his chest, then fell down dead. The power left me as quickly as it came, but I felt another presence. It was the Holy Spirit, there to guide me. I kept running. I ran and ran and ran, day and night for three days, without pain, before I reached the city of Catania and found a medieval stone convent on a hill off the town square. I knocked on the door, and as I entered the vestibule, I crumpled to the ground. The pain in my leg and hip was suddenly excruciating, and I could not take another step.

"Both were broken, and I was bruised, but the good sisters nursed me back to health and restored my faith in humanity. My faith in God was never in question.

"And so, young man, that is why I have my limp. It is my reminder of all that is evil and all that is good in the world. But, wait, there is a little more to the story. Because of the way Giancarlo died, I was afraid to go home. When the sisters at the convent took me in, I lied, just a little, and told them I was an orphan, beaten by a brutal and lecherous brother-in-law. So they protected me and taught me, and in time, I took my vows, knowing all along that I would have to leave Sicily someday and never return. When the order called for us to teach Italian immigrants in America, I was the first to volunteer. I had *made* myself the orphan I pretended to be and never returned home. I'm sure my disappearance became a great mystery in my village; one, thankfully, that never reached the convent.

"And that is my secret story, and I tell only you, and trust you to keep it secret."

I did, until now.

I ran home to record it the best I could, and I never again looked at Sister Lucia the same way. I now understood the root of her kindness. She learned to turn bitterness inside out, a holy approach. She taught with patience because she grew up with stupidity. She loved children because she had been spurned by her parents. She suppressed anger because she had been a victim of violence.

Her story not only changed how I saw her, it changed me. It was *her story*—with its dimensions of greed and lust, overcome by grace and virtue—that showed me the world was filled with people who had such stories to tell. You didn't have to travel the world to find them. They were right in front of you. It was a philosophy I adopted as a newspaperman.

The day after I recorded the story, I reread it, filled in some blanks, and made a little note on top, something I had never done before: *People carry their sadness like a wallet full of money: You can never tell how much they have just by looking at them.*

I thought it was clever then, and I still do, considering it was written by an 11-year-old.

But aside from that juvenile truism, I learned other things from Sister Lucia's story, although I didn't know it at the time:

The best stories have an element of confession.

The best stories shed light on a mystery.

The best stories say a lot about the times in which they occurred.

And the very best stories leave you wondering whether they are all true.

Was Sister Lucia telling the truth?

And how much of the truth?

Did she kill Giancarlo Graceffa? Was her lifetime of patient teaching a penance to win back God's grace for her pardonable crime? Or was there no murder, just a miraculous intervention for which Sister Lucia's life of good works was her way of spreading faith and giving thanks?

Looking back, I think Sister Lucia—who by her admission was not only capable, but adroit at lying—told me a fictionalized version of a painful story, although I can't decide if she sugar-coated it for my tender ears or made it more brutal as a way to show me my own orphaned life wasn't so bad. Either way, she was, at heart, a teller of moralistic tales, stories of survival and salvation, of faith and the rewards faith brings, no matter how circuitous and discouraging the route. In that respect, the truth doesn't matter. Only the moral of the story does.

So if I could ask her one follow-up question, it would not be whether the story was all true, it would be why she chose to tell me at that moment.

Did she see, in me, a need to hear it?

Or did she have, in her, a need to tell it?

Or was it a little bit of both?

I'll never know the answer. Sister Lucia retired two years after she told me the story, and years later, while I was in high school, word came in church that she had died in an old-age convent in North Jersey.

But there is one more thing her story taught me: Always listen to old people. Listen close enough to ask the right questions. History gives perspective, especially in a day when we are caught in technology-amped news cycles that spin like hamster wheels.

And this is where Fred Haines comes in.

1

Fred Haines was in an assisted living center when I met him in December of 1999. I was a feature writer for the *Shore Record*, the same plain-Jane local daily that had reported my father's accident some thirty years earlier.

I was looking for one of those end-of-the-century, witness-to-history stories. I figured I would go in, scout around, and find the most lucid old-timer. It didn't take long.

The Oceanview was a new facility—a Victorian facsimile of some of the grand, postcardesque homes built a century earlier along the coast. The address was Bradley Beach, but it stood five blocks from the beach and didn't even have an ocean view.

It instead overlooked a briny, stagnant pond edged with swamp grass and cattails called Fletcher Lake, named for a famous Methodist bishop. Bradley Beach was named after James Bradley, a Methodist who founded and built Asbury Park, which he named for another Methodist bishop. Both towns surround Ocean Grove, New Jersey's second summer resort after Cape May, built as a summer tent revival city for Methodists. I tell you this because the Methodists, who connected religious revitalization to God-given salt air and sea breezes, made the Jersey Shore the resort area it is today, though you would never know it.

The three towns once drew drinking water from the lake, but it had long been infiltrated with saltwater, just as the old, all-white Methodist towns were later infiltrated by Irish-Catholics and Jews and Italians, who eventually became rich enough and "white" enough to find their footing on the upward American stepladder. In Asbury Park, which began as a carefully laid-out American city, the ethnic whites were soon replaced by blacks during the post-World

War II migration north. The riots of the mid-60s hit the town hard, but in three short decades, the newly emboldened gay community found it a safe haven, and same-sex couples began to restore the beautiful shore town mansions wrecked by urban neglect, and opened restaurants and galleries. The down-and-out town of Bruce Springsteen was turning effete and chic.

Around the Oceanview were blocks of summer rentals—sagging, paint-chipped bungalows trashed by college kids each summer, then pieced back together by landlords each winter; an annual cycle of drunken fun for the lessee and runaway profit for the lessor. Closer to the beach were some new homes, mini-manses of varying styles. It would just be a matter of time before the bungalows would fall to new construction, existing only as mirages of good times in middle-aged memories.

The doors of the Oceanview parted for me and I stepped inside. It was cheery, with pastel hallways and shiny linoleum floors. The handrails were brass, polished to the point where you could see yourself in them. There were mirrors everywhere, reflecting light to make the place even brighter. This surprised me. I thought mirrors would be demoralizing to old folks—constant reminders they had become craggy caricatures of how they best remembered themselves. But that was Oceanview: clean, bright, and optimistic. I was expecting something more dismal, sadder, to match the decrepitude of the people I expected to find inside. I was wrong on both accounts.

In a solarium off of the front desk, a few residents gathered, faces pink, hair blazing white, in clean robes or casual clothes. A few gazed out over the pond, lost in thought or trapped in memory, but most were engaged in chatter. In a large mirror at one side of the solarium, I saw a gaggle of mostly women whooping it up in one corner, their laughter dominating the room. Then I saw myself: discount-store drab olive corduroy jacket over a light blue Oxford shirt, brown knit tie, un-creased khakis, and bargain-brand penny loafers. A reporter if there ever was one. I felt a twinge of self-consciousness among people so comfortable in their wrinkled skin.

I'd been in the business my whole life, right out of college, trying to follow in the boot-heel literary footsteps of John Steinbeck, Upton Sinclair, Sinclair Lewis, and Sherwood Anderson. The most sincere way to capture real American life, like Joseph Mitchell, Studs Terkel, and Gay Talese, I thought, was to write about it at the most base level—the daily newspaper.

Early on, I wrote the novelist Bernard Malamud a letter asking writing advice. He sent back a long note on a postcard, punctuated by one memorable sentence.

Learn who you are and write what you know.

I knew the Jersey Shore, so I stayed. Colleagues moved on to bigger papers, or television (and later websites), or teaching. Some went to law school, or into real estate sales, or onto other more lucrative livelihoods. I stayed put.

Of course, I was personally, painfully aware of the forced "paper-thinness" (an expression Fred Haines used) of much newspaper writing, beginning with the perfunctory, unsatisfying report of my father's accident. I knew I could be more thoughtful and thorough, and tell stories filled with meaningful detail that exposed motivations; stories that made enduring statements about the human character and condition, stories about tragedy and sudden loss, and how the spirit beats back both.

Armed with this high ambition, I came through the *Shore Record*'s doors with the same romantic notions held by every new reporter before me. To uncover—be it human drama or municipal corruption—and explain. To find a great story, and tell it well. Wrong, I was.

Like those before me, I was trained to gather scant information in the quickest amount of time and pound it into digestible newspaper stories; stories people would read and soon forget, excreted from their consciousness the minute something more pressing came up. But in 1999, I was still hopeful and was a smart reporter, and I knew the laughter I heard at the Oceanview signaled something special; it was unexpected in a place where death is a weekly visitor.

The old man at the center of the laughter faced away from me in a wheelchair. "OCEANVIEW" was stenciled in white against dark blue, reminding me of one of those Hollywood "DIRECTOR" chairs. The laughter I'd heard was from the people around him. Robust cackling is the best way to describe it. The "director," dressed in fresh blue-gray flannel pajamas covered by a clean royal blue robe, was the center of attention, holding court.

I watched for a few minutes, as he gestured with his hands to punctuate a story. His voice was clear and stable and loud, in that hard-of-hearing way. He sat tall in the chair, a head above the people around him. Some of the women were rolled close to him and touched his arm at each punch line.

"Oh, Freddy, you are too much!" one said.

As I moved closer to hear him, I was intercepted by an oval-faced Jamaican nurse in a lemon-lime striped smock.

"May I help you?"

I told her who I was and why I was there, and then asked, "Who is that man?"

"That is Mr. Fred Haines. He was a reporter, like you."

"Could I meet him?"

A lazy wave said, "Follow me."

"Mr. Haines!" she shouted, her Jamaican lilt spiced with an official tone I thought was designed to mock me. "Mr. Haines, you have an *important* visitor."

"A what? Oh, good!" Haines said, wheeling toward me. Now I saw his face; the prominent nose and tightness in the cheek of a lean man, a strong jaw protruding to the same plane as his forehead. A ladies' man now, and in his day, no doubt.

I introduced myself and gave the reason for my visit.

"A newspaperman! Me, too. Was, anyway. The *New York Daily Mirror*. It's gone now. Oh, boy, I musta known you were coming, 'cause I was just warming up, telling my friends a few stories from the old days."

"Oh, Mr. Haines! Why you gonna lie to this man?" the nurse said with a dramatic scoff. "You make it sound like that's not what you do all day. You and your stories!" Turning to me she said, "He's our 'round the clock entertainment. You'll see."

The old folks around him took the cue, rising slowly and unsteadily from their armchairs to shuffle off. A woman patted his arm as she left. "See you at lunch, Freddy."

Haines wheeled up closer. "Still got it. Ninety-three, and still got it."

He winked, then reached into his robe pocket and pulled out a pair of industrial black-rimmed glasses. Then he looked up with comically magnified eyes; I could see my own refracted image in the lenses.

"Well, well," he said. "Let's see our newspaperman. Why, hell's bells! You're just a baby! I thought she said you were a reporter, not the paperboy!"

"I guess I'm older than I look. To you, anyway," I said, with my best disarming smile, and stuck out my hand. We shook, and the hard veins on the back of his hands wiggled under my fingertips.

"Hah! Good one! A ball-buster, I like that. Reminds me of me. And you're right; it's all relative. Just like my lunch dates. Who ever thought I'd be looking forward to eating with an 80-year-old broad! Hah!"

***

More than a decade has passed since that day. I am no longer a newspaperman, which I owe mostly to Fred Haines. When he was done telling his story, I knew the paper could never contain it, like so many subjects and stories these days. I filed my perfunctory witness-to-history story before the odometer flipped from 1999 to 2000, but we stayed friends. In the end, he gave me his story, and I gave back something everyone should have near the end of their life: someone to listen to it. When I told him I was going to write his whole story, a book, he suggested I call it *Jersey in the '30s*.

"Lousy alliteration, but I like it!" he said.

Jersey in the '30s was the where and when for four major international news stories: the Lindbergh baby kidnapping, the fire on the ocean liner *Morro Castle*, the *Hindenburg* explosion, and Orson Welles's "The War of the Worlds" broadcast. Fred Haines covered them all. Jersey was his beat.

"Right place, right time," he said. "Simple as that. That, and the old Haines luck. Let me tell you something about luck, kid: You make your own. You show up first and stay latest, and that's how you get the best stories."

Another title he liked was *Bruno's Confession*, the title of his own unfinished manuscript.

"That'll hook 'em," he would tell me later. "Nobody knows Hauptmann confessed but me. And now you. You can tell the world and lay the controversy to rest."

According to Haines, Bruno Richard Hauptmann confessed to him that he'd killed the Lindbergh baby. The confession came in a jailhouse interview just weeks before Hauptmann went to the electric chair.

In his earlier days as a tabloid guy, Fred Haines would have run from that interview screaming "Stop the presses!" But by the time of the confession, he had changed. Something inside him had broken, and something else was getting fixed. As a newspaperman myself, I understood this. You become a proprietor of others' grief and misfortunes, and it's a disgraceful job at times, yet every now and then it offers a chance for redemption. Fred Haines took that shot at redemption. He kept Hauptmann's confession a secret for almost sixty-five years.

The question, you ask, is "Why?"

The answer—what else? To protect a woman—Mrs. Hauptmann.

And did I believe him?

Yes. Because the day he told me, more than ten years ago, I saw in his face what I had seen in Sister Lucia's: a flash of conscious wrestling behind the eyes, then the resigned look of inevitable confession. Those expressions were quickly followed by the same faraway look Sister Lucia gave me when she patted the chair and said, "Let me tell you a little story."

In Haines's magnified eyes was a watery depth of grayness that made me realize this old man had a story, a real story, to tell. His eyes were deep pools of experience, Scottish lochs of old secrets waiting to burst through an ancient dam, a flood of emotions racing down a spillway to me: stories of pain, of loss, of confession, just as with Sister Lucia. And he wanted to tell this story not just to anybody, but to someone who could absorb it and learn from it.

Suddenly, I knew there was something Fred Haines *had* to tell *me*. He had a secret of his own.

2

"**P**ush me down to my room there, young fella. I got something I want to show you." The wheels squeaked as we rolled down polished linoleum floors, Fred Haines directing me through the rights and lefts of the Oceanview's halls. His veiny hands were lazy on the chair armrests, his thin shoulders relaxed against the vinyl chair back, just inches from my gut. I felt a caretaker's affection for him in that moment. I was in his service.

He had me wheel him to his bedside cabinet where he yanked open the veneer walnut door with enough force to make the attached vanity mirror vibrate.

"Here, do me a favor," he said. "Reach in there. See those folders? I got my best clips in a manila—*inamanila*! Hah!—folder. Folders. Pull 'em out."

"Any one in particular?" I asked.

"Hell, it don't matter! They're all good!"

There were three, overstuffed like paper tacos and held tight with thick, red rubber bands.

"Take those rubber bands off for me," Haines said. "My fingers don't have the strength anymore. All those years punching the typewriter."

I put the folders on his bed, a standard hospital electric model with a veneer headboard that matched the cabinet, and snapped off the rubber bands. Haines wheeled up and opened the folders. He peeled off the top few pages and held them up to scrutinize inches from his magnified eyes, like a jeweler looking for flaws in a diamond. He then waved them in front of my nose, chirping with glee.

"Here it is, the first few days of the Lindbergh baby story," he said. "Oh, boy! This was history being made, and I was part of it!"

The clips were brown and brittle, but straight as pressed leaves. There were hundreds of them. Full front pages of the *Mirror*, the stories from inside. Months and years worth, from LINDBERGH: THEY STOLE MY BABY to BRUNO GUILTY! and all the ones in between:

GONE WITHOUT A TRACE
PLEASE BRING OUR BABY BACK
NATIONWIDE DRAGNET
LAST GOODBYE FOR LITTLE LUCKY

"That was my idea, to call the baby 'Little Lucky,'" Haines said. "It added to the tragic irony, don't you think?"

The headlines kept coming, blurting out names of people long forgotten, but known in all American households during the case:

HOW NOW, BETTY GOW? ... a story about the Lindberghs' Scottish nanny who was grilled by police.

DR. CONDON'S GRAVEYARD SHIFT ... a story about a ransom drop by one Dr. John F. Condon in a Bronx cemetery as Lindbergh waited in a nearby car.

And on and on.

Haines began laying them out on his bed, building a patchwork quilt of newspaper clips.

"There you go, my boy, all right in front you, the Crime of the Century. And all written by me, alias Frederick G. Haines."

He pulled out a front page of the *Daily Mirror* Extra with a photo of a shoulder-to-shoulder crowd packed onto the street outside the courthouse after Hauptmann was convicted, a sea of gray suits and fedoras.

"Lookit there," he said, pointing to a man on the courtroom steps, near the front door. "That's me. And there's Mrs. Hauptmann. The crowd drove her back inside, the poor thing."

I looked close. Sure enough, it was Haines, captured by a photographer, his youth preserved for all time. His features were sharp, even in the gray, matted newsprint. He stood out, taller than most around him, a thin man in a double-breasted suit. His arm was reaching out toward Mrs. Hauptmann, but she didn't seem to notice.

"Yep, I was there, all right. Boy! Those were the days ..." he said, not at all wistful, but thrilled he had lived them. "Tell you what. Take 'em home—but be careful—and read 'em, then come back tomorrow and we'll really talk."

***

That night I read most of his clips, amused by his dramatic and occasionally mawkish writing style, but recognizing a rhythm and balance that allowed the stories to flow easily. There was *voice* in the writing. As I read, I imagined a young Fred Haines, fedora perched on an angle, cigarette dangling, clacking away on an Olivetti, keeping time with the sharp-edged words in his head. The voice was New York wise guy in the '30s sense, a side-of-the-mouth voice of inside information. The voice was tough and abrupt and hurried, but very, very cool. The voice had swagger. Like it or hate it, it was a voice—something most papers no longer had.

My own place, the *Shore Record*, lost its voice after the founder died. For 70 years, it had been a family operation, begun by Benedict Smith, a wire factory worker who made a fortune by inventing the machine that forged narrow strips, then cut and twisted them into paper clips. He had a factory in Newark, a mansion in East Orange, and a summer place in Long Branch called a cottage, but as large as his winter place. In the mid-1920s, Smith started the *Shore Record*, divesting himself of stocks to do so, a move he would describe as "dumb but lucky" for the rest of his life. Smith believed industry gave every American a chance to be an inventor; he deplored investors and stock market men who built their fortunes on other people's initiative. The voice of his paper cheered on the middle class in its pursuit of the American Dream. Politically, it backed populists but would expose them as hypocrites if they failed the voters. It had a simple slogan: *Fairness.*

"Fairness is what we Americans strive for," Benedict Smith once said. "Freedom is a byproduct of fairness."

When he died, his son took over, changing the slogan to the *Shore Record: A Sure Thing.* The paper became more picture-oriented and big on sports. The weighty old stories bolstering economic growth and social enlightenment were tossed for a more "reader-friendly" approach. Shorter, lighter stories. And crime. And more crime. It stood for nothing. Certainly not fairness, as stories about politics became stories about politicians and not the people they supposedly served.

When I went to work there, circulation was 156,000 and sinking like shells through seawater—swirling, but steady in decline. The Smiths were now part of the market rich and sold the paper to Sinnott, a public company that began in billboard advertising and became one of the country's biggest newspaper chains. The company returned double-digit profits to shareholders by cutting, then cutting more. News space and staff shrunk. The surviving staff at the *Shore Record* had their own new motto: "The Sure Wreck: All the News That's Fit to Print on a Billboard."

Reading old Fred Haines's articles gave me clarity on something I already knew: Old-style yellow journalism didn't create the public appetite for prurient stories, it fed it. It made it acceptable. It made money by appealing to the masses. The American Free Press ideal guaranteed in the Bill of Rights—that the press had a fundamental role in protecting citizens against a tyrannical government—began its slow death, as Fred Haines would admit, "in Jersey in the '30s." My paper was just late to the game.

"Guilty as charged," Haines said when I visited him the next day. "We gave the people what they wanted. Razzamatazz, and all that jazz. No apologies."

He was shaved close, all pink and scrubbed clean, waiting to shine. His hair, white and waxy, was combed perfectly. He had gotten *ready* for me. I remembered a line from an old song:

> *You look like a still,*
> *from Cecil B. De Mille*

So here was Frederick G. Haines, ready for his close-up. We spread the clips around the bed, and our photographer took a few pictures of him. In some he smiled; in some he was pensive. In some, he held up a clip near his face, in the unnatural way family members hold up pictures of murder victims for newspaper photographers and TV cameramen.

And then it was just me and him.

***

"Let me dispatch with the necessary details, son, so's you don't have to ask a lot of unnecessary questions.

"I was born in 1906, down on Vecsey Street in Lower Manhattan, back in the days of wood-frame apartment houses and piles of horse shit on the streets. You know, that was our big what-they-call 'environmental problem' nowadays. Back then we just called it horseshit and watched our step. Hah!

"I was born at the perfect time for a man of my talents—too young for World War I, a little too old for World War II, and just right for the New York tabloid newspaper wars of the 1920s and '30s. We entertained readers through the high times and the Depression. Took their minds off things. I mean, what do you think people would rather read about? Government financial policies to tame greed on Wall Street, or a lust-driven love triangle murder involving some financier? Like any good newspaperman of my day, I knew how to manipulate the facts to satiate the public's taste for lurid detail. People complain about the news being sensational today. Hell, I helped invent it!"

He wheeled over to his cabinet again and opened the top drawer.

"Let me show you my prized possession."

He pulled out a newspaper page encased in plastic food wrap.

"This was the most famous *Daily News* cover ever. Ever! Bigger than JFK getting shot. Bigger than Man on the Moon, or Son of Sam."

The full cover was of a woman, with a hood over her head, strapped to the electric chair.

"That's Ruth Snyder. Back in '27, she took up with a corset salesman named Judd Gray and, well, I guess she liked the way he tightened her laces. Before you know it, they conspired to bump off Mr. Snyder. Then they got caught, squealed on each other, and next thing you know, Ruth Snyder is getting the chair. First woman, and last, fried in New York. Ever."

Haines was just a kid then, barely 21, but he covered the case, trial, and execution as a "runner," chasing neighbors, investigators, lawyers, and, finally, jurors for details and quotes. The paper sent him to Ossining to witness the execution, just after New Year's in 1928.

"My job was to phone in the details to the regular reporter back at the office, who would dash off a story for an Extra. And I made the best of it, I tell ya. Nobody ever heard of a metal detector, so I was able to strap on an ankle camera. The photographers back at the paper showed me how to use it, and sure enough, I got the shot of Mrs. Snyder getting the jolt. And here it is."

He handed me the newspaper cover. It was fuzzy, with a blur of movement, almost like a modern freeze frame from a surveillance video. The woman's head was tilted back, her body stiff. Haines let me see it for a couple of seconds, then snatched it back and put it away.

"Jesus Christ, you shoulda heard the noise! Everybody calling us sleazeballs, bloodthirsty even."

Haines said the *New York Times* wrote an editorial calling the picture "offensive" and "vulgar." So did the *Herald Tribune* and *World*. They all decried the "eroding standards of the high-minded practice of journalism," he said.

"They weren't offended—they were jealous of our sales! That edition of the *Daily News* with Mrs. Snyder getting zapped sold 2 million more copies than normal, and we couldn't print enough. The presses ran all day, and the papers flew off the newsstands like a tornado hit town and got snatched out of the newsies' hands before the ink was dry on their mitts. They sold like ice cold lemonade in hell."

Haines stopped and wheeled himself to the window. It overlooked the west end of Fletcher Lake, where an old brick pump house and rusted pipe system, long defunct, were crumbling from neglect.

"There was another picture," he said, with a sudden loss of altitude. "Another bad one. It was of Little Lucky. That one I didn't keep. That one I never wanted to see again. That one ruined my life. When it was all over, I figured that was my comeuppance for Mrs. Snyder. Penance is more like it. What goes around comes around, like they say, and it came 'round and bit me, but good."

He became silent, then closed his eyes. I let him sit for awhile, enough to wonder if he'd fallen asleep or was just deeply engaged in a conscious dream of some long-gone consequence.

A few minutes went by.

Finally I said, "Do you want to tell me about it?"

The question didn't startle him. His eyes remained closed. "Not yet."

A moment later, he opened his eyes suddenly and spun his chair toward me. "What I want is a cup coffee. Let's hit the dining hall—get a change of scenery."

In the pastel-colored cafeteria, a woman brought us two cups and a metal coffee urn. "Great, darling," he said to her, "'cause we'll be here all day."

His mood upturned with the caffeine.

"Best if I start at the beginning. See, I was born to be a newspaperman. Literally. My pop was a pressman at Pulitzer's *New York World*—hah! Say *that* three times fast!—so, I had newspapering in my blood. When I was little, I'd sit on his knee, looking at the fresh paper he made every morning, the ink still damp and muddy on his fingers. It must be strange to hear an ancient-timer like me talking about my pop, but I remember him like it was just yesterday. His passion for news was contagious. He read me stories from all over the world, faraway places with names that don't exist now. His reading opened up the world for me, and, as I got older, I fantasized about discovering that world in a tramp steamer—up the Nile, down the Amazon, across the China Sea—filing dispatches from exotic places. Funny, how, in the end, I found the biggest stories of my life right here in Jersey."

The family lived in Lower Manhattan, just a few blocks from Newspaper Row, where the city's great old dailies lined the street like competing department stores; the *Times, Sun, Tribune,* and *World* were all there, cozied up against City Hall, the police plaza, and the courts. The newspaper businesses housed everything from offices to printing plants. When the presses ran, the streets vibrated under wagons and Model T trucks and newsboys who descended on the block to deliver and hawk the papers. Pulitzer's building with its cupola tower threw a shadow over the rest. It was one of the tallest buildings in the world at the time.

"Believe me, it was Pulitzer's way of saying, 'I'm the big boy on this block!'" Haines said.

In those days, everything that mattered was downtown. The papers, the government, Wall Street, even the theater district. Downtown was the center of New York, and therefore the world.

"When you turned up Park Row, if you didn't feel alive with energy, you were dead," Haines said. "Everything was young and marvelous."

He closed his eyes to recapture it.

"The stone stanchions of the Brooklyn Bridge looked like castle turrets over Downtown," he said. "Fulton Street took you down to the fish market, where Portuguese and Spanish fishermen argued with Jewish wholesalers in whatever passed for English. Nassau Street was the financial district, where you'd find the pocket-watch set. Broadway was two blocks away, where car backfires set horses to whinnying, and the smell of cloudy blue gas exhaust mingled with the stench from steaming piles of manure on the cobblestone. The Battery was a few blocks south, where you could see the green rises of Jersey and Staten Island, the far-off horizon of the harbor, and Lady Liberty, looking out for the immigrants. Canal Street, Chinatown, Little Italy—all less than a mile north. The world came to Lower Manhattan, and the Park Row newspapers ruled that world."

Haines's New York was a land of infinite energy and unlimited possibility.

"What a time that must have been," I said, thinking how the country had lost its momentum.

"There was never a better time in America, you betcha," he nodded. "Everything was happening and *fast*."

"And you ran right along," I offered.

"Damn right. Either that or get trampled."

Haines said his father loved the news business and wanted him to get into the "clean hands side of it."

"He figured that was the order of things over here. You know, the son doing better than the father. So he got me a job as a copy boy at the *World* after high school, and I did that for a year or so. His dream was for me to become a big deal columnist, the kind of guy who *everybody* that's *anybody* reads in the paper—a talk-of-the-town kind of guy who gets recognized on the street, in the saloons, and in the swankiest restaurants."

Haines began to sing, "*East Side, West Side, all around the town …*

"Before Pop died—a heart attack in the middle of a bulldog run—he'd talk about how it would be a Great American success story. The son of an ink-blackened mechanic growing up to be a feared and respected columnist, rubbing—and throwing—elbows with the white-glove set.

"From his view in the basement pressroom, my pop probably thought the starch-collared reporters and editors upstairs were intelligent, responsible, and honorable, and would give me a fair shake to make it in their world.

"Luckily, he died before he saw that the Pulitzer editors—mostly Ivy snobs—weren't too keen on seeing a pressman's son with his own byline. I hustled, and I could *write*, but I stalled as a copy boy at the *World*. Every time I asked the white-shirts for a promotion, they told me I could make more money in the pressroom or in paste-up."

Haines got his break with the tabloids, the first of which had been started by Joseph Medill Patterson, grandson of *Chicago Tribune* founder Joseph Medill.

"Young Patterson had an eye for newspaper mischief—and money—so he started the *Illustrated Daily News*. They were hiring, I was going nowhere at the *World*, so I jumped ship and got hired as a reporter, and just like that, I was a tabloid guy. And once a tabloid guy, you couldn't go back."

"There was that much of a distinction?" I asked.

"You know anything about ladies' dresses?"

"No, I guess not. Why?"

"There's three kinds of ladies' dresses: designer, designer knock-offs, and budget. The guys who make and sell the middle and bottom shelves can make a fortune, but they can never ascend up. The guys at the top think they have the corner on taste and don't let anybody else in. Well, that was the newspaper business in my day. Tabloid guys were the bottom rung. We made as much and sold more, and we were better street reporters, but we weren't in the same league as the *serious* journalists, the way they saw it. No established broadsheet like the *Times* or *Herald Tribune* would ever hire a tabloid guy—hell, they thought we were lowlifes and street hustlers. We hustled, all right, all over town, all over stories."

"The line is more blurry now," I said.

"That's because no paper stands for anything anymore. Back then, every paper had an identity. Today, they try to be all things to all people and end up doing nothing well. I took pride in being a tabloid guy. And I was a damn good one. There wasn't a story I couldn't sniff out or write with pizzazz. And it paid off."

Patterson dropped *Illustrated* from the masthead a few months after Haines came on board, but it was the only thing that dropped. *Daily News* circulation started strong and kept climbing.

"We had a formula to satisfy the public's blood-lust for crime and sex-lust for gorgeous girls," Haines said. "We chased death, from mob rubouts to street crime to automobile crashes. We were always first to photograph gruesome scenes and best at writing lurid details to match. Those pictures usually ended up on Page 1. On Page 3, we ran our daily beauty contest and put half-bare girls in the paper almost every day.

"Crime and passion! Sometimes, if we got lucky, we'd get both: a beautiful girl murdered! Or better yet, a beautiful girl murderer in cahoots with her lover—a *femme fatale*, like Ruth Snyder."

What came next, Haines said, was a flood of tabloid knock-offs. "Other millionaire megalomaniacs, like William Randolph Hearst, got the idea to start tabloids, putting us tabloid guys in high demand. And when you're in high demand, there's money to be made. I ended up at the *Daily Mirror*, which Hearst started in '24. It was filled with celebrity gossip, scandal, and true crime—all hued in deeper shades of yellow than his already-sensational *New York Journal* broadsheet.

"I called him 'Wilhelm Adolf Hearst' because he was a Nazi sympathizer, no matter what they say. I know it for a fact. A lot of American big shots, including Lindbergh, thought German industry and technology would rule the world and wanted to jump on board. Today, they call it globalization. Back then, we called it what it was. *Greed*. Greed first, America second. That's the American way! Hearst ordered his editors to either ignore or doctor stories about Hitler. I know. Later on, I worked for the guy, and my story about the *Hindenburg* was one of them."

Before Haines went to work for the *Mirror*, he had been lured to the *Daily Graphic*, a scandal sheet owned by a fitness guru named Bernarr Macfadden.

"Nobody remembers him these days," Haines said, "but what a character! Macfadden was an old-time muscleman, an exhibitionist who liked to pose in nothing but a grape leaf. His stomach was like a washboard, and he had biceps like bocce balls. He'd sworn off meat and spent hours a day doing calisthenics and isometrics, which he claimed to have invented. One thing he *did* invent was his own religion. What did he call it? Cosmo ... Cosmo ... *Cosmotarianism*. He believed only the musclebound would reach heaven. I guess he envisioned the Great Beyond as something like the Sistine Chapel. Who knows, maybe he was right—it's as good a theory as any. The Bible says God made us in His image, but you can bet God is no scrawny string bean or fat slob." He grinned. "At least not according to all those *EYE*-talian Renaissance painters!"

Haines told me how Macfadden started a magazine called *Physical Culture* in 1899. Articles about new diets and exercise regimens, and other miraculous reshaping techniques were wrapped around daring pictures of nearly nude men and women showing off their physiques. Basically, the fitness infomercial of the Victorian era.

"It was scandalous for the day," Haines said, "but Macfadden defended it as a 'human art form.' Whatta bunch of baloney. It was a nudie magazine except for the leopard skin briefs on the men and skimpy bathing suits on the cuties. Sold like crazy."

The next of Macfadden's ventures was *True Story*, a confession magazine that was basically the daytime soap opera of the Victorian era. Then came *Movie Mirror*, the precursor to supermarket "celebrity-sniffers," as Haines called them.

"Up till then, the movie mags were all controlled by the studios. The studios handed out press releases they wanted printed, doctored photographs of their stars for publication, and kept the seamy side of showbiz—parties, sex, booze, and narcotics—out of the mags.

"Macfadden had other ideas. He went the scurrilous gossip route, and to hell with the studios! He had an army of 'contributors' in New York and Hollywood, running the streets and hiding in shadows like nocturnal rodents, chasing the 'it girl' or leading man of the moment to catch 'em in a compromising position. The photographers, especially, were star-stalkers. They prowled the speaks, camped out at club entrances and in hotel hallways, ready to pop some celebs' privacy with a flash of the bulb. Macfadden's

Movie Mirror was the first mag to print these kinds of candid shots—and paid good money for them! As the Law of Economics dictates, where there's money to be made, people run over each other to make it. Macfadden's willingness to buy these pictures started the industry of thug-photogs—bullies and hustlers who'd stomp your grandma to get a shot of some blonde starlet's backside. You call 'em paparazzi today, but they got their start with Bernarr Macfadden. Like Valentino said, we Americans build up stars only to tear them down. And Macfadden's mag was the wrecking ball with the biggest swing.

"He was a nut-and-berry eater who abhorred booze, coffee, and tobacco. Some newspaperman! But while he preached clean living, he helped turn the minds of millions into mashed turnips with the garbage he printed."

This was a history lesson for me. I thought of celebrity culture as a creation of the modern, desperate media. In the late '80s, Sinnott began a flimsy Sunday insert magazine for their papers called *Stars!* It had a thrown-together, scrapbook look; a subliminal message to readers that they were getting the very latest in gossip, fashion, and celebrity lifestyle. It was almost all photos: snapshots of celebrities of every variety caught working, playing, vacationing, exercising, smiling, scowling, showing skin, dressed to the teeth, doing anything but looking ordinary. The captions all touted the subject's latest movie, TV show, or recording, or gave some other tidbit about their personal life and couplings. There were no real stories, just lead-ins to thematic picture montages like "Shop Hopping on Rodeo Drive," "Hot Jock Workouts," and "Nightmoves at Sundance."

The advertisers loved it. *Stars!* was a moneymaker, and Sinnott started up a separate brand, selling spinoffs at supermarket checkouts for a buck. *KidStars! TeenStars! MovieStars! TVStars! PopStars! SportsStars!* The only thing missing, we joked, was *PornStars!* But, in truth, those junky tabs kept papers like the *Shore Record* somewhat afloat. Without them, there would have been deeper cuts, if not extinction. That was 20-some years ago, long before the internet and 400-channel digital TV. The explosion of shock (or schlock) gossip since has been, well, nuclear.

I said to Haines, "Amazing how Macfadden's name has been lost, considering."

He nodded vigorously. "In the early '20s, he started this big muscleman contest at the Garden, the winner claiming the title of 'The World's Most Perfectly Developed Man.' It was vintage Macfadden, right down to the hyperbole. Well, the first year, a nobody named Charles Atlas wins. The second year, Atlas wins again! Macfadden was no dummy. He realized he was creating a monster, so he cancels the third year. But he was too late—Atlas had already knocked him off the block as the country's most famous muscleman. He came up with his own version of isometrics, called Dynamic Tension, and started his own mail-order company. You know the ads I'm talking about—the 97-pound weakling getting sand kicked in his face by the beach bully."

"Sounds like Macfadden was a casualty of the revolving-door celebrity culture he helped create," I said. "Famous today, forgotten tomorrow."

"Everybody credits Andy Warhol with the '15 minutes of fame' line," Haines said, "but guys like Macfadden and his henchman, that bastard Walt Winchell, started it back in the '20s."

"You knew Winchell?" I asked.

"Knew him, and hated him. And the feeling was mutual. But I'll get to that. Let me tell the story …"

3

Macfadden wanted reporters who weren't afraid to peek in windows, sift through garbage, or trespass in the morgue to get the most sensational story or picture.

"I was fresh off the Ruth Snyder coup, so Macfadden sent a bunch of his boys to talk to me.

"'What do you make?' they asked.

"'Forty bucks a week,' I told 'em, which was a lie—I made thirty-five.

"'Mr. Macfadden will double it,' they said, which was a lie, too, because they ended up paying me sixty-five. Still, they didn't have to ask twice."

Haines jumped to the *Daily Graphic*, and the first thing he did was change his byline from Fred Haines to Frederick G. Haines.

"I thought it sounded more sophisticated ... worthy of a man on his way up, making sixty-five bucks a week."

"So, what does the 'G' stand for?" I asked.

"George. Gerald. Geronimo. Whatever you want, see, because it stands for nothing. I don't have a middle name, but a middle initial gives you more ... hell, more *authority*. Like a university president or executive producer. I thought it gave me class."

"But why 'G'?"

"Mainly because I liked it—a muscular sound between two softies, 'Fr' and 'Ha.' That, and I had a baby sister—she's gone 25 years now—and she used to call me *Fredgy* because she couldn't quite pronounce *Freddy*. It stuck with me like a sing-song lullaby all those years later. Fred G. Fred G. Fred G. ... Frederick G. ... Frederick G. Haines. I thought it had a nice ring to it. Still do! When people used to tell me they didn't believe anything they read in the papers, I used to think, 'Damn right!' Even my name was a goddamn lie! But all these years later, that name is linked forever to the news of the day. That byline says, *'and you were there!'* like Cronkite used to say on that show from the '50s. That byline gave me lifetime ownership of a lot of history. Owned by me, loaned to a world full of readers!

"Now, what was I was saying … ?"

"You were telling me how you went to work for Macfadden," I offered.

"Right! And let me tell ya, what a rag the *Graphic* was! Like those supermarket tabloids you see today but without the aliens. Hah! We hardly covered serious news at all. No, we covered the wreckage of the human heart. Love triangles, lovers' murders, lovers' suicide leaps, women wronged by Romeos, geezers wiped out and left broken-hearted by dance hall floozies. We loved first-person tales of woe. *He broke my heart and left me broke … I thought she was my Queen of Hearts but I ended up the Joker …* Problem was, most of these sad sacks couldn't write a lick, so the reporters ghost-wrote them. That was my specialty, at first. Let me tell you, I could wring tears out of a dry towel. But nobody was crying for these saps. They were laughing at them! What we wanted was for your average Bensonhurst housewife to yak about it over the clothesline with her neighbor, *'Well, I read in the* Graphic, *blah blah blah …'* How stupid can you get?!?"

It was, I thought, the Roaring '20s version of reality TV. We're not crying *with* you, we're laughing *at* you.

Haines then told me about "nuisance suit" stories. Hat-check girls who sued millionaires for "alienation of affection" after one night stands. Wall Street brokers accused of cheating financially unsophisticated widows. Uptown doctors botching a minor surgery and killing some poor schnook with 10 mouths to feed. They all made for great headlines. And they all got settled quickly out of court the minute they hit the papers.

"So you got justice?" I asked, hoping Haines took at least one step on the high road.

"Justice, schmustice. It was entertainment! All of it."

The other big thing for the *Graphic* was movie and stage stars. Most of the names are meaningless now—"on the scrap heap of celebrity," Haines said. "But in those days everyone wanted a peek under their sheets."

He rattled off some names and gossip from the day. Were Earle Larimore and Lynn Fontanne, stars of *Strange Interlude*, lovers off Broadway? Was Emil Jannings, a big silent film actor, returning to Germany because he was afraid of the talkies, or because word was out he was a "pansy"? Were Mary Pickford and Douglas Fairbanks's famous Hollywood parties *really* wild, Romanesque orgies?

"What the readers wanted to know, pardon my French, was who was screwing who," Haines said. "Like we could tell them! Everything was second-hand gossip picked up from cabbies, doormen, and bellhops. For a buck, these 'sources' would answer yes to the most preposterous questions, and tell you the most outlandish lies."

"So the truth ..." I began.

"Truth, schmuth—the truth didn't matter!" he said. "Who cared if it was true, anyway? It was *entertainment*! Now, I never understood why your regular working Joes and Janes cared so much about these celebrities who could not have cared less about them. In fact, for the most part the stars of that era treated average citizens with contempt when they encountered them in daily life."

Haines paused for a moment.

"Here's something I never understood. What did those Joes and Janes think they were reading? Did they *really* believe they were getting authentic, intimate details about their false idols? Did they *really* think a newspaper like the *Daily Graphic* even *knew* the truth? What we printed was no more than rumor and innuendo."

Haines explained that this was how Walter Winchell got his start. His gossip column at the *Graphic* zeroed in on stars from Broadway and Hollywood, along with politicians, financiers, and gangsters of the day. The column was syndicated; he got a radio show and eventually became a bigger celebrity than most of the people he wrote about.

"On radio, he became a jingoist, and people took him seriously," Haines said shaking his head. "It was all America *this*, America *that*—what a phony! It was an act. He didn't care one iota about regular people. Hell, he didn't even know any! His nose was always pointed up the social ladder, never down. And he sure as hell didn't speak for the average American."

"Nothing has changed but the technology, bringing more voices to the free-for-all," I said. "The hard-right and hard-left showmen today who claim to know what real Americans want are the tools of political operatives, partners in creating angst and polarization—and all for what? Their own celebrity. The critic, desperate to be as famous as the creator. The news messenger, striving to be bigger than the newsmaker."

"That was Winchell to a T," Haines said. "But there's one thing I'll never get: He had this gravelly, irritating voice that made you want to reach down his throat and pull out his Adam's apple. For the life of me, I never understood how the guy made it in radio—I guess Americans are gluttons for punishment."

Yet, Haines admitted, for better or worse, Winchell was a media pioneer. He was America's first gossip columnist and the original radio manipulator.

"Never forget, he got his start in vaudeville," Haines said. "He was an actor first and a first-class jerk, right from the start. He let everybody know he was going places, and something in the way he talked said, 'And you ain't.'"

Haines and Winchell took an immediate dislike to one another.

"When I came to the *Graphic*, I had Ruth Snyder under my belt, so I was going places, too, I figured. Well, Winchell thought there was only room for one *Übermensch*. I tried a few times to be friendly. One night, I said, 'Hey, Walt, let's get a drink.'

"'They wouldn't let you into the places I go,' he said, not even looking up from his typewriter.

"Boy, that rankled me."

Later, when Winchell was famous, he had his own table at the Stork Club and an entourage of bodyguards and ghostwriters.

"When he was on top, people would flock to him like it was a chance to kiss the Papal ring," Haines said. "But in the early days, when it was still Prohibition, nobody gave a damn about Winchell. He'd go to the swanky speaks and stand around like a pimply-faced wallflower at a prep-school dance."

One night, Haines and a bunch of other reporters were having a drink at a speakeasy called Paddy's, which he remembered as a dark, airless place down by the Fulton market, made darker by the fog of cigar smoke. A place where they threw peanut shells on the floor.

"We were at a table up front, when Winchell came in and walked right past us without even a nod. Well, I'd had half a snoot and wasn't going to let that pass. I caught his eye in the long mirror behind the bar. He looked away, like I was invisible, so I announced, 'Well, well, fellas, look what the cat dragged in. The Great Walter Winchell.' Well, Paddy's was a dock joint so nobody even looked up from their beers to see what I was talking about, which gave the rest of the boys at the table a big laugh. Winchell looked away again, and even though it was dark, I could see his neck stiffen. So I goaded him some more.

"'Whatsa matta, Walt ol' boy,' I yelled, 'The Stork closed for fumigation?'

"Again, the boys laughed. They didn't like Winchell any more than I did. Winchell put down his drink and came to the table and hovered over me, his face getting redder by the second.

"'Shut your fat mouth, Haines,' he hissed. 'I'm meeting a tipster, and I'm trying to be discreet. I would prefer that none of the cretins in this bar recognize me.'

"'Oh, so that's what you would prefer, is it?' I said loud. 'Hah! Who the hell'd recognize you? Besides, this is a place for men who do real work, not fairy actors and show biz shills who slip you a fin to get their name in the paper.'

"'If they could read, they'd know me,' said Winchell, keeping his voice low.

"'If they could read, they'd throw you out for abusing the language,' I shot back. That got the boys going again, and Winchell knew he was losing face fast.

"'You know, Haines, some day your mouth is going to get you in big trouble,' he said. 'You're crossing the wrong guy.' His face was boiling red.

"Now, there was some truth to that. Word was Winchell palled around with Owney Madden, a Hell's Kitchen thug who got control of the New York booze flow with the help of some Lower East

Side dagos. On top of that, Winchell was gathering a storm cloud of power at the paper. But, hell, I couldn't let *that* guy intimidate me. I fashioned myself as a bit of a roughneck, while Winchell was a reed, beefed up only by the shoulder padding in his suit jackets. Like I said, I'd had half a snootful, and by now the whole bar was watching—it was as quiet as I'd ever seen that place.

"I jumped up, yanked him close by the lapels, and gave him a little shake. He got this frightened puppy-dog look in his eyes, which made me shake him harder.

"'And your mouth is going to be missing a coupla teeth in a minute,' I said, shaking him a few more times.

"And you know what the Great Walter Winchell did then? He farted. Sure as hell, this big, loud, involuntary fart escaped his ass. Hah! The boys just about died laughing. I looked over at them and back at Winchell, and said 'Jesus Christ! You didn't mess yourself, did you, Walt? Hey, boys, I didn't even have to slug him to knock the crap out of him!'

"Now the whole bar busted out laughing, and the boys were doubled over with tears running down their faces, and Winchell, for once in his life, was speechless. He was yammering something, and I shook him one more time, then slapped the fedora off his head.

"'Don't ever tell me I'm crossing the wrong guy,' I said, full of bravado. 'Now, get out of here before I turn you over my knee and give you a spanking.'

"I knew this hit Winchell where it hurt, because with his wool, houndstooth three-piece suits and black-band fedoras, he tried to look like a real hardened pro, but the fact is, he was only a couple of years older than me, and I was 23 at the time.

"'You haven't heard the last of this, Haines,' he finally managed to say. When he leaned over to pick up his hat, I gave him a quick boot in the ass, just for good measure.

"The whole place erupted—*erupted!*—in laughter."

The next day Haines got called into the editor's office, where Winchell sat.

"He wanted me fired but had to settle for an apology. It was the most fingers-crossed handshake I made in my life.

"After the boss was satisfied that we'd buried the hatchet, Winchell brushed by me on the way out and muttered, 'You'll get yours,' out of the side of his mouth. But in no time, he was the biggest thing in New York, looking at guys like me fading off in his rearview mirror. I figured that was that. Pretty soon, Mr. Wilhelm Adolf Hearst made him an offer of—get this!—five hundred bucks a week to join the *Mirror* and off he went. I was happy to see him go. And let me tell you, I was stupid to be happy. With Winchell gone, circulation at the *Graphic* dropped like a wounded bird."

Within two years of Winchell leaving, Haines said, Macfadden had "bled enough red" and shut the paper down. Haines tried to return to the *Daily News*, but was rejected. We don't like traitors, he was told.

"How do you like that? Here I was, the guy who made their most notorious front page, and they wouldn't take me back. You know, years later they decorated the fine china in the executive dining room with famous *Daily News* front pages, and you would cut your Chicken Florentine or London Broil over the image of Mrs. Snyder being sizzled. So there I was, part of the *Daily News* legend, and they wouldn't take me back!"

The *Mirror* gave him a job working the night police beat.

"And my old buddy Winchell, he fixed me, but good. He convinced this mealymouthed, square-headed city editor named Rudolph Dicks that I was a crumb-bum. Dicks wouldn't give me the time of day, let alone a half-decent assignment. He put me on the late night shift, covering liquor store hold-ups, run-over jaywalkers, and frozen stiff Bowery bums. He took great sport in sending me all over the city—up to Riverdale in the Bronx, out to Flushing in Queens, down to Gravesend in Brooklyn—on wild goose chases.

"Always, it was the same thing—'Hey, Haines, we hear a widow got murdered in Canarsie. A sweet grandmotherly type. Go check it out.' I'd take the subway there, walk in circles looking for some phantom address, find the local precinct, and have the cops tell me they had no idea what I was talking about."

One cold March night in 1932, Haines was bundled in his overcoat, feet on the desk, smoking a cigarette, doing "absolutely nothing but watching the clock tick. March was coming in like a starving lion, and the *Mirror* newsroom was cold and drafty and empty and lonely. I was blowing smoke rings and watching the plumes ride, widen, then dissipate on wafts of cold air, all the while thinking, 'Up in smoke, just like my career.' It was dead-time in Newspaper Purgatory, the time of night when it's so quiet you can hear the faint hum of your inner ear."

The clickety-clack of the Teletype machine startled Haines. He heard Dicks swat the copy boy's feet off the desk and say, "See what that is, will ya?" The boy ripped the paper out of the machine and handed it to Dicks.

Dicks read it and got a funny smirk on his face.

"I could tell he was about to fling me far into the night," Haines said, "much to his sadistic delight.

"Then Dicks said, 'Hey, Haines, you know anything about Jersey?'

"'I got an uncle who lives in Jersey City,' I said.

"'He got a car?' Dicks asked.

"'Yeah ...' I said.

"'Well, go over and borrow it,' Dicks said, 'then drive out to some podunk town called Hopewell. It's probably a hoax, but it says here somebody's just kidnapped Charles Lindbergh's baby.'"

4

"Listen to this," Haines told me. "*When celebrity replaces knowledge, there are grave implications for the future.* Know who said that?"

"No. I don't."

"Richard Nixon, that's who, when Jane Fonda went to Hanoi to side with the Reds during Vietnam," Haines said. "He was probably still burning over his loss to Jack Kennedy, the first television-celebrity president. Still, it's a quote for the ages, especially this one."

I should have guessed. I knew some history, and "grave implications" was used by Nixon's boss, President Dwight Eisenhower, when he warned against the military-industrial complex taking over the American economy and conscience in his farewell address. Nixon saw the "grave implications" of the celebrity-entertainment complex coming and put the blame square on the media, which was erasing the line between useful news and related entertainment. Was Jane Fonda going to Hanoi for news, or entertainment? Was what some actress said about the war important information, or self-serving opinion? That was just the start. Forty-some years later, was the American conscience finally rendered unconscious? Were we now "dumbed-down," as we used to say in the first days of the failing newspaper business?

"And here we are," I said to Haines.

"And here's where we came from," Haines said to me. "Let me tell you, there never was, and never has been, a celebrity like Charles A. Lindbergh. He was the first, what you call today, *multimedia* celebrity. Newspapers, film reels, and radio were competing for the public eyes and ears, and news was exploding as an industry when Lucky Lindy came along, with his single-engine *Spirit of*

St. Louis and his five cheese sandwiches packed for the trip, and his Midwestern aw-shucks good humor masking his aloofness."

What Lindbergh did was remarkable, Haines said, but the technology is what made him world famous.

"Think about It. How many people back then knew what Julius Caesar looked like? Or George Washington? Or Christ himself? When Lindbergh landed, every person in every country in the world with electricity got to see his face and watch him move through the crowd. At that moment he was the most *seen* man who ever lived."

Fast forward 90 years. Internet, Twitter, Facebook, cell phone cameras, omnipresent video. Technology, not meaningful accomplishment, leads to fame. The entertainment complex and the communications gadgets built around them run the culture, grave implications be damned. Haines was right about Lindbergh. He was the first.

"Let me tell you something about Lindbergh," Haines said. "While nobody could have been prepared for the celebrity that engulfed him, nobody could have been less prepared for it than he was. He was a backward guy with a genius for nuts and bolts, but with the social grace of a hammer. He was shy and mechanical. Clumsy even. A stiff, if you want to know the truth. Hell, I'm not sure the guy had a girl before Anne Morrow, because even with all his fame and money he was never hit with a paternity suit, and that was big business in those days.

"He was aloof, very private—and that's what made him game. That's what put the sport in it for us news guys! All he wanted was to be left alone, and the more we tried to get to know him, the more he tried to hide. The more he tried to hide, the harder we tried to get to know him. A vicious cycle of hunter and prey, 24 hours a day. He was the first sacrificial lamb on the Altar of Public Adulation."

Haines grew philosophical.

"Lucky Lindy kept just out of our reach, sailing above us in low clouds laced with ocean spray, flying somewhere over the Atlantic … surrounded in blackness, alone as any man has ever been, in a place where bravery conquers stupidity and ambition trumps common sense.

"And then the baby got kidnapped, and he crashed back to earth."

Haines then asked me to take him back to his room. "I started a book about the Lindbergh case, but never finished it," he said as I pushed him down the hallway. "After all was said and done, I didn't feel worthy."

It was an odd statement, and I asked him to explain. He shook his head. "It's complicated."

Back in his room, he opened the drawer of his bedside table and pulled out a bundle of typewritten pages wrapped in plastic. He handed it to me: his unfinished manuscript.

"Take a minute and read," he said. "Read it out loud. I want to hear how it sounds."

I began.

BRUNO'S CONFESSION

People always ask me if Bruno Hauptmann was guilty, and I say "yes" because I know he was.

But I also say it didn't matter. Guilty or not, Hauptmann was doomed the minute they arrested him, because "when celebrity replaces knowledge," everything else—like justice or reason—goes out the window!

And that's what the Lindbergh baby case was all about.

It was Lindbergh's celebrity that got his baby kidnapped.

It was Lindbergh's celebrity that led to the ham-handed investigation that followed.

It was Lindbergh's celebrity that whipped public fascination into near hysteria.

Lindbergh's celebrity overpowered the case. How the police investigated, how the prosecutors prosecuted, how the defense attorneys defended, and how we newspapermen reported the story.

And I know.

I was the first New York guy on the scene, and I stuck with it almost to the bitter end—for almost three years, from the day the baby went missing until the day Hauptmann was convicted and thrown in jail. I knew that case top to bottom. The back door deals, the behind the scenes blundering, all of it. More than I'd like to, truth be told. And now, I'd like the truth to be told.

The enduring question from the case is "Was Hauptmann really guilty?"

I know he was, but that's not the point. The point is this: The "story" dictated he was guilty, and Lindbergh's celebrity dictated the "story." In the end, the case wasn't about facts; it was about the "story."

Bruno Richard Hauptmann, with his swarthy complexion and guttural one-word protestations, was the perfect villain, pulled right from the Book of Antagonists. He was an anti-Christ, pitted against the sainted Charles Augustus Lindbergh—a man elevated by the world public for his amazing flight across the Atlantic, then beatified because of the momentum of his celebrity.

Hauptmann, innocent or guilty, was cast to perfection. He was a dark, brooding Kraut at a time when America was getting edgy about Germans and their mysterious American Bund Societies, with their Klan-like bonfires and secret pledges popping up all over the place. So he was a coward, sneaking away in the dark with the courageous aviator's namesake, a helpless innocent.

In the early '30s, the slaughter of World War I was still fresh in Americans' memories, and Germans were still immigrating in droves. Americans lumped them all together: The Kaiser, Hauptmann, and later Hitler—it didn't matter. It was in their arrogant Aryan blood to be ruthless, to spill the blood of innocents, to enforce their view of the world and their vision of superiority.

Being guilty didn't make Bruno Richard Hauptmann evil. I don't think he killed that baby on purpose; he probably fell. It was an accident, a kidnapping gone awry. It was the press who made him evil. We even gave him a villain's name. Bruno. Of course, everybody who really knew him, including his own wife, called him Richard, which was his middle name. But when we newspaper guys cornered him like a pack of German Shepherds, we stuck the name "Bruno" on him for life and history.

Hauptmann was perfect as the Prince of Darkness—just as Lindbergh was as the Prince of Light: blond and brave, strong and silent, standing tall and courageous in the face of a personal and national tragedy.

Charles Augustus Lindbergh, with a name part king, part emperor, part farmer, came out of nowhere to compete for the Orteig Prize—a $25,000 purse for the first crew to fly non-stop between New York and Paris.

After New York hotelier Raymond Orteig put up the prize in 1919, more than one aviator died trying to win it. Down went French flying ace René Fonck with a crew of three. Richard

E. Byrd, the first man to fly over the North Pole, crashed on a test flight. Two Frenchmen, Charles Nungesser and François Coli, joined the roll call of Orteig dead just a few weeks before Lindbergh's attempt. These men were all famous flyers.

Then along comes Lindbergh, who was little more than a barnstormer, with his Minnesota plain-goodness and his Missouri backers, and nothing between his daring youth and tragic death but a sputtering engine. And he says he's going to do it alone. Is he in it for money? Is he in it for fame? No, he says, he's in it because his Midwest practicality tells him it can be done—especially by a man flying solo.

Solo, because human blood isn't gasoline, and if your engines run dry, all the co-pilots in the world aren't going to save you from going into the big drink. Lindbergh's idea was to throw everything he deemed not essential overboard, including the radio, parachute, and navigational equipment. It was a suicide mission, and the nation was invited to watch. He first flew solo from San Diego to New York to test his new plane, using a Rand McNally railroad map to navigate.

He made it. He landed alive!

Haines interrupted my reading.

"You see, the kid was *perfect* for us news guys. Minnesota farm boy and son of a hayseed lawyer turned congressman. Army-trained pilot who barnstormed at state fairs throughout the Midwest. American as amber waves of grain. Plain enough to be Everyman. Lucky enough to become Superman. We made him into a comic book hero, and there wasn't a damn thing he could do to stop it.

"Keep reading."

The masses flocked to Lindbergh as soon as he landed in New York. The newspapers branded him "The Flying Fool" because he was going to go across the Atlantic alone. The papers watched his every move, detailing everything about the flight. His mother came to wish him good luck, and the papers turned her fare-thee-well kiss into a farewell kiss. Under the headline THE LAST GOOD-BYE?, the Daily News ran a comical photo of Mrs. Lindbergh bussing him on the cheek while Lindbergh had a "gee whiz, ma!" expression of blushing embarrassment on his face.

This went on for a couple of days, as Lindbergh waited for the weather to clear. Reporters and newsreel guys camped out at the airstrip on Roosevelt Field. The morning he flew off, Lindbergh was kept awake all night by a newsmen's card game in the hangar where he was trying to get some shut-eye. That began a love-hate relationship between Lindbergh and the press. We loved him, he loved hating us, and with good reason. Eventually, we loved hating him, too.

Lindbergh escaped the media horde early the next morning by climbing into his single-engine Wright Whirlwind, firing her up, and running away down the runway. The plane, filled to the brim with fuel, lifted off like a pregnant dodo bird, barely clearing some telephone wires at the end of the airstrip.

As Lindbergh disappeared into the dawn fog, the world heard the news: The Flying Fool was airborne. They tracked him up the Atlantic coast, over Providence ... Halifax ... St. John's.

When he disappeared off the coast of Newfoundland and into the black night, the world held its breath. And when he was spotted over the Irish Isles at daybreak, the world let out a sigh of relief.

And when he touched down at Le Bourget Field outside Paris a day and a half after he took off, the world celebrated the accomplishment as yet another testament to mankind's relentless conquering of the unconquerable. Some likened it to Columbus discovering America, only more daring because Lindbergh did this alone.

Columbus or not, one thing is certain, none of the other American big shots of the day—Babe Ruth, Jack Dempsey, Douglas Fairbanks—none of them could hold a candle to Lindbergh in terms of international appeal or recognition. Live radio and newsreels covered every moment of it. Anticipation became frenzy—nobody ever mobbed a movie star or a president like that. He had to be rescued off the field at Le Bourget, the crowd was so thick. Men and women alike tore at his clothes, in a crush just to touch him. He was whisked through the streets of Paris to the American Embassy, through crowds fit for a king. But Lindbergh was bigger than a king. He was a god in the mythological sense. He cheated Death, he beat Mother Nature, he overcame Mother Earth's geography, and he skirted Neptune's graves.

He made the world smaller overnight, something even Columbus couldn't do. He flew and stayed afloat, over darkest depths of ocean and emptiest heights of sky, like a leather-jacketed angel who got closer to death and closer to God than the rest of us ever could. There was something Christ-like about it; he ascended into the heavens, invisible to all earthly eyes, and then came back.

That's why the world fell at his feet. Calvin Coolidge sent a battleship to France to bring him home, Congress pinned the Medal of Honor on him and made him a colonel, the French decorated him with their Legion of Honour, presidents and kings hosted him, money and jobs were thrown at him. He was a millionaire before his ears stopped popping. And he was only 25 years old.

I looked up from the manuscript. "Pretty amazing," I said.

"Even more amazing," Haines added, "is that it didn't die down. This was no fly-by-night fame. Lindbergh continued to fascinate people for years as he criss-crossed the country and the world in his airplanes, a goodwill ambassador exploring and navigating the globe. When he finally married, he and his wife stayed on the *tour de goodwill* and became the public's eyes and ears to the newly opening world of exotic adventure in far-off corners never reached by ship or car.

"These days, people throw the word *icon* around. Every dead actor or actress or pop star is called an icon in the press. But Lindbergh defined the word. He was the symbol of American ingenuity and guts and restlessness at a time when the country epitomized those characteristics. And his 'story' is one for the ages, because what the story is *really* about is the sins of the culture of American celebrity!"

Haines sat straight up in his chair.

"Sins of shallowness, sins of stupidity, sins of callousness. Sins of the press," he said with a mournful earnestness that took me by surprise.

"Let me tell you, when the Teletype machine at the *Daily Mirror* office spit out the words, 'New Jersey State Police say baby son of Charles Lindbergh has been kidnapped,' I grabbed my phony New York Police Department badge out of my desk drawer, and I was on my way. Anything 'Lindbergh' was major news—even if it was just a hoax.

"And when I got a cab to Jersey, and emerged from the Holland Tunnel, my life would change forever. For the better, then worse, then eventually better again, I guess. At least I'm still here to tell about it."

As soon as Haines got to New Jersey, he knew the report was no hoax. Police had set up roadblocks and were checking all vehicles headed to New York.

"The place was thick with cops and lit up like the Fourth of July. I jumped out of the cab and cut through the stopped lines of in-bound cars and their smoky exhaust fumes that lingered like a low fog. I went over to a Jersey City cop and asked what was what. 'Get the hell out of here,' he said.

"Now, I was smart enough not to ask him if it was about the Lindbergh baby, because I would have been cuffed on the spot, dragged downtown, and rubber-hosed until I admitted I stole the kid."

Instead, Haines used his phony badge on a Jersey City fireman who was shining a fire truck spotlight into cars as police searched each one.

"The fireman told me it was something about Lindbergh's baby," Haines said. "Kidnapped, he guessed, because the cops were looking for somebody who didn't look like they should be traveling with a 1-year-old.

"I found a phone outside a diner and called Dicks. 'It's true,' I said. 'They've already got roadblocks up leaving Jersey.'

"'Then whaddaya waiting for?' he screamed at me. '*Get out there!*'"

Haines walked a dozen blocks to his uncle's house, near the Hoboken border. It was about one in the morning. He knocked, and, in a few minutes, the lights blazed.

"'Uncle Chuck, I need your car,' I told him. 'Charles Lindbergh's baby been kidnapped, and I have to get to a place called Hopewell down by Trenton.'

"And you know what? It was probably Lindbergh's celebrity that made Uncle Chuck turn over the keys, no questions asked."

5

Uncle Chuck had a black 1929 Chevrolet Coach—nothing fancy. The Coach was to Chevy what the Model T was to Ford—a utilitarian car for the proletariat—except that '29 Chevys were the first mass-produced six-cylinders. Uncle Chuck called his Coach the "Lucky 6" because he bought it with General Electric stock he'd cashed in a few months before the Crash of '29. He'd spent years bolting doors on ice boxes in the GE factory in Newark and didn't believe in playing stocks as a rule. A man has to work for his money, Uncle Chuck always said. But when he saw other factory guys making money on GE stock, he figured "Why not?" and bought in.

"Well, when the market fluttered in March that year, a few months before Black Thursday's October nosedive, Uncle Chuck cashed in his stock and bought the Lucky 6 for $595 cold cash. Sold GE and bought GM, he liked to say."

Behind the wheel of the black Lucky 6, Haines began his trek across New Jersey to Hopewell, a mountain and valley town a few miles north of Trenton.

"Let me tell you, I was feeling anything but lucky. Truth is, I was scared. I knew every alley and back alley of New York; I knew where the drunks sprawled and muggers lay in the shadows. But New Jersey was dark and wide open. I had no idea where I was going, except into the teeth of a nationwide dragnet. I made sure all the car's papers were in order, because I knew I'd hit roadblocks on my way to Hopewell. I was even smart enough to have Uncle Chuck write me a note, saying he let me borrow the car for a trip to Philadelphia to visit a sick aunt. It was a good thing we had the same last name, and I had him sign his name—Charles W. Haines—exactly as it looked on the registration."

Lindbergh had discovered Hopewell and the hilly woods around it during a flyover, Haines told me. Weary of being pestered by press at his in-laws' mansion in Englewood, he decided to build a mountaintop retreat on Sourland Mountain. The house was not quite finished, but it was livable and the Lindberghs were spending weekends there.

"What irony!" Haines said. "The baby was snatched from the one place Lindbergh thought his family would be safe."

In those days—Jersey in the '30s, as Haines liked to say—the main road between New York and Philadelphia was the two-lane Lincoln Highway. It connected cities like a train line, but it was built over old stage routes. From Jersey City, Haines drove to Newark and through the industrial swamplands by Newark Bay, through the medium-sized city of Elizabeth and into the suburbs; Linden, Rahway, Colonia, Iselin, Menlo Park—where Edison invented the light bulb—Metuchen, Highland Park, one after another like "whistle stops," Haines said, and into New Brunswick, "the college town."

"I was stopped three times by local police. There were always two cops on these stops. Each time I explained my business—the baloney about the sick aunt—as one would shine a flashlight in my face, ask questions, and study me for lies, while the other would shine his light around the car, open doors, and look under the seats.

"The closer I got to Hopewell, I thought, the more roadblocks there would be. Hah! Was I wrong about that."

Past New Brunswick, New Jersey was no-man's land, "strictly Sticksville," Haines said. Nothing but Haines, the Lucky 6, and the darkness. No cops, no other cars, no streetlights.

"It was now at least four in the morning, the black heart of a black March night, and I could see nothing but flatlands. When I went around a bend, my headlights would jump off the road and shine on some rundown Mom-and-Pop fruit-and-vegetable stand with a sagging chicken coop out back. The towns had hick names like Three Mile Run and Rocky Hill."

Outside Rocky Hill, Haines turned off Lincoln Highway and followed a sign to Hopewell. It was a deep-back-country road, gravel and dirt in most places, nothing like the evenly paved Lincoln. The flatlands gave way to hilly forests, and the road narrowed, wound, and dipped.

"My headlights bounced up and down, often hitting nothing but woods. A few times, I slammed on the brakes, thinking I'd hit a dead end. There were deep drainage ditches on either side, and the late winter thaw had turned them into rushing streams. The dark before dawn lurked outside the Coach like an alley mugger, and the car lurched over potholes and quivered in gusts of wind. I drove slow, knowing a blowout or skid into a ditch would leave me stranded in that godforsaken place. A few branches snapped down on the car, scaring the bejesus out of me as they rapped against the roof or ricocheted off the windshield. I remember thinking, 'If Lindbergh wanted to get away from it all, he sure as hell found the right place.'"

As Haines told me this, he had his eyes closed tight as if to shut out distraction and recapture the scene. He paused a moment, then abruptly opened his eyes.

"I'm old and frail now," he said, "so I don't mind admitting this, but I never felt so scared and alone in my life as I did that night. I was a city boy, used to lights and people … and there, in the middle of nowhere, I felt like Lindbergh must have felt on his flight, groping through the darkness in uncharted territory."

He became quiet for a minute. When he began to talk again, his voice was more subdued and his words more measured. It was for dramatic effect, I thought, to get me to pay close attention.

"I remember thinking that somewhere out there on this cold, windblown night was Lindbergh's terrified baby, crying to feel the warm bosom of his mama. Let me tell you, at that moment, I felt the same way.

"And let me tell you something else: It wasn't just the woods that had me scared. It was the story, too. It was bigger than big, the biggest thing I'd ever worked on. In a few short hours, the world would wake up to the news. They would rush out to buy morning Extras and afternoon papers to read all about it. I would be the eyes and ears for millions of those people. To be honest, all the baloney with Winchell and Dicks had staggered my confidence and now, in the middle of nowhere, I was wondering if I still had the old Haines's swagger. I'd dreamt of a story like this my whole life, and, now that it was here, I wondered if I was up to it. Was I the old Haines—the blood-and-guts tabloid king—or the guy killing nights blowing smoke rings in the city room, a guy going nowhere *slow*?

"Oh, I was a nervous wreck. All those thoughts made my bowels gurgle like a vat of acid about to explode. I was sweating in my overcoat, even with the cold wind whistling through the door and window seams of the Coach. I wanted to pull over and relieve the pressure in my bowels, but I wasn't stopping out there for nothin'

… nothin' short of a baby in his jammies shivering in the middle of the road."

After a few more miles, Haines saw a lightened sky through the bare trees on the mountain.

"It looked like dawn, but I was headed west. It was Lindbergh's estate, all lit up by searchlights."

He found a dirt road heading up, then another, then another.

"I was zigzagging up the mountain, headed toward those lights. I had to get my nerves under control. 'It's *showtime*, kiddo,' I said to myself in the rearview mirror."

"Showtime" was an old trick Haines learned from a veteran Broadway actor named Paul Gillespie. Gillespie drank to subdue his stage fright most nights. So before each performance, he was either drunk or scared to death. Either way, it didn't matter. Minutes before the curtain went up, he'd stare at himself in his dressing room mirror and say, "Showtime, kiddo," over and over again until the actor in him took hold, and the character he was playing took over from the drunk or terrified Gillespie.

"I kept looking at myself in the mirror and pulled the brim of my fedora down to eyebrow level, feeling less and less like a scaredy-cat named Freddy and more like a tough-guy reporter named Frederick G. Haines. It was showtime."

Haines had done the same thing at the Ruth Snyder electrocution and at a couple of gruesome murder scenes, including one that involved two children stabbed by a father distraught over his cheating wife.

"It was like acting, being a tabloid reporter," Haines said. "I would remove myself from something horribly real and pretend I was some character in a detective story. Not just me, but the cops, the suspects, even the victims. Especially the victims. I had to remind myself of this as I approached the Lindbergh estate. Baby or no baby, I had to remember my Cardinal Rule: Victims are merely characters in a newspaper story. The mother's grief ... the father's anguish ... nothing more than a day's entertainment for the readership. Human grist for the newspaper mill."

"That seems a little cold," I said.

"That's how we did things in those days," he said. "That doesn't make it right. It just was."

"But what about your own empathy?" I asked. "Didn't you feel like you were exploiting people?"

"*Empathy*? Empathy, outrage—whatever—was for the readers. My job was to tell the story."

"You mean exploit the story," I said flatly.

"Call it what you want," Haines said. "I called it my job."

***

At the estate, Haines bluffed his way in. A young Hopewell cop stood in the middle of the dirt road leading up to the house. Haines pulled out his phony NYPD badge, flipped it out quick, then back, like a real pro.

"'Haines, NYPD fingerprint guy,' I said.

"'Go ahead, sir,' the yokel cop said.

"The house was a good mile off the road, and the spotlights were my guide. All the fear had left me. All the elements that rattled me earlier—the cold, the wind, the darkness—now just boosted my adrenaline and added to the adventure. There was a new element, too. The woods were crawling with cops with flashlights, scouring the grounds for evidence."

Here, Haines closed his eyes again, and the old photographs in his memory came into focus.

"Then I saw the house, new and freshly whitewashed, illuminated by spotlights. It was in a clearing, sticking up like a glowing iceberg on a black sea. The house was a sturdy little fortress, made of stone and stucco, with high angled peaks. It belonged where it was built—in the middle of a forest. Detectives in trench coats and Jersey state troopers in their blue soldier's field jackets and riding breeches were all over. I kept my ears open, my mouth shut, and my notebook hidden while I moved in and around clusters of detectives, picking up bits and pieces of conversations.

"Cops gossip like school girls, and they stood around one-upping each other with details. Hot details that hung in the cold air like the vapor of their breath as they talked. Sweet, copious details that would appear within hours in the *Daily Mirror.*"

Through his eavesdropping, Haines learned that a ransom note had been found in an envelope on the radiator in the baby's room on the second floor. Demanding $50,000, the note was written in lousy English, probably by a foreigner or someone trying to pass himself off as one. He also learned that a ladder had been found in the woods—a homemade contraption that folded three ways and had one broken rail. A wood chisel and a set of man-sized footprints were discovered below the baby's window. Some of the police went into town, to rouse laborers who worked on the house, Haines said, while others were on their way over "to the nuthouse in Skillman" to see if all the "fruits and vegetables" were accounted for.

But for Haines, the biggest news was that the Lindberghs weren't even supposed to be in Hopewell that night. They had extended their weekend stay because, Haines said, "Little Lucky had a sniffle." Only the butler, the housekeeper, and the baby's nurse would have been aware of the change in plans. It pointed to an inside job.

"I found all this out in no more than 20 minutes, just moving around the cops like I belonged there," Haines said. "Confidence is a great disguise, my friend. Act like you belong anywhere, and pretty soon, you do! I don't care if it's a crime scene or a society wedding, if you play the part with confidence, you're in!"

He asked me for the unfinished manuscript and shuffled the pages to find another place in the story. "Here. Read this."

Around back there were some alcoves left in the shadows made by the spotlights, and I ducked into the darkness to surreptitiously write up my notes. While I was there, I peeked into windows of the house, writing what I saw. The house was crowded, with uniformed cops and guys in suits in every room, talking quietly, in hushed tones like you hear at a wake. I recognized Colonel Henry Breckinridge, Lindbergh's attorney. He was talking in the dining room to a state police officer, who I later learned was Colonel Norman Schwarzkopf, the commander himself. Both Breckinridge and Schwarzkopf were lean and dignified and slightly gray. Both were ramrod straight, the kind of men ready to lead the moment duty called—whether they knew what they were doing or not.

At the kitchen window, I saw the housekeeper and butler, both Irish-looking, making coffee for detectives, their every move being watched by a couple of troopers.

The next window was by the breakfast nook. The room was not as brightly lit as the others, but I could still see plenty. There was a man and a woman—the Lindberghs! He was standing behind her, his hands on her shoulders. She barely came up to his narrow shoulders and was dressed in a dark robe. She was pressing a hankie to her face. No beauty, this Anne Morrow Lindbergh, but alluring with her deep-set, dark eyes. Her chest was heaving, like she was gasping for air.

Colonel Lindbergh, Lucky Lindy himself, was dressed in a gray suit, no vest. His large head was tilted, chin up. He looked out over her, stoic, as if trying to find a point on the horizon. She sagged into him, and he stiffened, maybe even pushed her away a little. He said something. I couldn't read his lips, but there was no tenderness in his expression. I was hoping to see him wrap his arms around her, kiss her tears away, and try to soothe her—so I could write it—but he never did. Instead, he turned away from her and walked back toward the dining room, which was being set up as "Command Central."

I continued to watch the woman sobbing, all alone, and it hit me that she was already in mourning. Her mother's intuition told her the baby was not coming back. Her despair moved me—I felt ashamed for watching her, but I was paralyzed. I knew I was seeing her bare her deepest emotions. In this moment she didn't have to appear strong for her husband, or the police, or the public. And I was the only witness.

I took down some notes with the vision of an "Anne Morrow's Sorrow" Daily Mirror exclusive in my head. Rereading my words, I realized they were vapid. How does one describe the black agony, the emptiness of such deep grief?

Haines interrupted me. "Where are you?"

"The part on 'Anne Morrow's Sorrow,'" I said. I told him I was moved by it, that it made me think about my mother's despair after my father's death and how she never recovered.

He asked me some questions, and I told him about coming home to a house where sunlight was shut out by closed blinds, except for slivers of light that came through the slits. I remembered her cigarette smoke, illuminated blue, as it hung in those strips of light, a slow moving cloud of gas, at once peaceful and toxic. This was her life, such as it was. Once detached from her expectations, she closed herself off to new possibilities, and, in the end, what she died of was not grief, but loneliness.

Haines nodded. "For me, there's nothing as gut-wrenching as a woman—a mother or a wife—in mourning. That's why I never wrote this part of the story. I decided Anne Morrow's raw grief—on that night, anyway—should not be made into a public spectacle."

"What about your 'victims are merely characters' credo?" I asked.

He shrugged and squirmed a little in his chair. Suddenly, he seemed weary.

"Hell, I don't know," he said, with resignation. "Maybe I was just incapable of describing it, or maybe it was too complicated—too far off the script of the stoic Lindbergh persona. Whatever it was, I left it out and convinced myself it was my secret act of kindness to her. One that I later undid in spades."

"Tell me."

"Not now—I'm tired. Keep reading."

After I watched her for a few minutes, I made my way around the house to the three-car garage, where New Jersey State Police were setting up a communications center and had already installed a batch of fresh phone lines. I walked quick, like I was on official business, went right to a phone, and called Dicks back at the Mirror *office.*

"You better have more than 'it's true,' because that's all over the radio," he said.

I laid it all out for him. All the details, everything I knew. Every time I dropped another juicy detail on him, all he could say was, "Jesus Christ, this is great, Haines! Jesus Christ, this is beautiful!"

Then I hit him with the color. The ghostly mansion and the wind-whipped woods and the police siege on the estate.

And then I dictated these words: "In a private moment in the breakfast nook of the mansion, away from the prying eyes of the police who overwhelmed the house and grounds, the gallant Colonel Lindbergh, dressed in his trademark gray flannel suit, comforted his grief-stricken wife with tender words and a gentle kiss. Mrs. Lindbergh, still dressed in the night clothes she wore when she first heard that her only child had been taken, seemed to draw on her husband's strength."

I stopped reading.

"It was a lie," I said.

"Yep. But it was a better story," Haines said. "I mean better for the sake of public ingestion. Lindbergh was a hero. Nobody wanted to venture into the gray areas of his personality. They wanted it simple. In black and white. Nobody wanted the truth. It was only the first night, just hours after the baby vanished. And already the story had a momentum of its own."

6

Haines repeated that he was tired.

"We'll talk some more tomorrow," he said. "I don't have the wind I used to."

I stacked his yellowed, brittle news clips and put them away for him.

"All these years," he said, "and the story still holds up. It was one for the ages."

I asked if I could take the manuscript home. "Sure," he said, "it'll save me telling you all the details."

My apartment is a few blocks off the beach in Belmar, overlooking the Shark River Inlet, the waterway into a 50-dock charter fishing boat marina. A few times a day, in morning and late afternoon, the steel-girder bascule bridge of the Jersey Shore rail line opens to let the boats glide through. Cars go over the inlet on a new, higher bridge that carries Route 35. It wasn't until after I moved in that I realized I could see the curve where my father crashed from my small balcony.

The early 1970s building is boxy and brick-faced, put up in a hurry with no time or thought for character. Demand was high then; people leaving Asbury Park like refugees after the riots of 1968 needed places to stay. On the night I returned home with Fred Haines's manuscript, I was struck by the parallels. He kept his life's work in a cabinet by his bedside; my own clips filled a plastic bin. Neither of us had anyone to care about all those stories once we were gone. They would be tossed in a dumpster without a thought for the characters in them or who wrote them.

It hit me that, maybe, I could rescue this man's story. I sat down to read without another human voice to interrupt me. It was all

Haines. He wrote it just like he told it, his distinctive voice coming through clear in the narrative.

The morning after the baby was kidnapped, Lindbergh's estate was overrun by packs of salivating newsmen—those who didn't have the means or nerve to find the place in the middle of night like I did.

Most came by train to Princeton or Trenton and took a cab out to Hopewell. They swarmed to the estate, all wanting to be part of this macabre event, and traipsed around the crime scene and trampled possible evidence.

The three-ring atmosphere made Schwarzkopf nuts enough to scream at a subordinate, "Get some control of this!" He turned on his heel and ran smack into a Pathe newsreel guy who had been filming him.

"Get the hell outta my way!" he yelled, shooting the subordinate daggers before storming off.

The cop he'd screamed at was a state police captain named Henning, a big, angular guy who looked like a cleaned-up Frankenstein's monster, truth be told, though he was reduced to a puddle when Schwarzkopf blew up at him.

I saw my opening. Like old Benny Leonard throwing a left hook off the jab, I pulled Henning aside and introduced myself.

"Mind if I give you some advice?" I asked. Henning didn't answer, so I kept going. "Best way to get control is get rid of the reporters. Best way to do that is to understand they're mostly a bunch of lazy dogs. So give 'em a place to go—a press headquarters, a place where you guys spoon-feed them information with regular briefings. Set up something in town where they're all staying, and that'll keep them off the estate."

Henning gave me a muddled look. I could see his wheels spinning as he tried to figure out why I wanted to help.

"Who gives the briefings?" he asked finally.

"Schwarzkopf. Breckinridge. You. Anyone with authority who knows what's going on. Trot out Lindbergh himself once in awhile to keep the dogs at bay."

Henning thought some more.

"How will this keep reporters away from the house?"

"Most don't have cars. They came by train. They have to hitch rides or pay cabs to come up the mountain. You'll be making their lives easier, which is what they want. Like I said, they're a pack of front-porch dogs, one lazier than the next. Trust me, Schwarzkopf will think it's a brilliant idea."

"You might have something there," he said finally.

Henning was sold, and so he sold it to Schwarzkopf. And it was a brilliant idea—and worked out brilliantly for me. Within hours, state police set up a press headquarters at a freight depot in town, rounded up the reporters and drove them down. Me, I stayed close to Henning, my new ally. Now I had two huge advantages over the rest of the news bums—not only did I have Uncle Chuck's car to get up the mountain, I had Henning in my hip pocket.

Because Schwarzkopf loved his idea of booting the press, Henning was brought into the inner circle. Let me tell you, there are two kinds of cops. The surly, aloof type, and the kind that blab like small-town housewives over the clothesline. Henning looked like the first, but once he got to know you, he could yammer with the best of them. The only thing he loved more than being on the inside was showing off that he was. So when he gave up secrets, it wasn't for me. It was for him. For his own ego.

I was set. I had my mole in place and my competition corralled. The cops there were used to seeing me, so I continued to blend in, careful not to ask too many questions. I'd been in front of the story from the start, and now I'd made damn sure it was going to stay that way.

The plan worked beautifully because the press bums were content to sit on their asses and wait for handouts. Like this: One day Mrs. Lindbergh released the baby's food likes and dislikes, so the kidnappers could feed him right. There was Schwarzkopf at the train depot, talking about strained peaches and mashed bananas. Another day Lindbergh himself came down and handed out an open letter to the kidnappers begging for the baby's safe return. In each case, the nation's newspapers built their coverage around this pap.

Not me.

With Henning feeding me, I broke one story after another. Oh, I loved nothing more than walking into press headquarters, slapping a Mirror *with my latest scoop down on the table and saying, "Here you go, boys, read all about it in the* Daily Mirror, *before you 'hear' it from your editors."*

As I read this, I felt wistful for a time I never experienced. There was no competition in my newspaper world, no chase on the big story. The *Shore Record* had outlasted a daily up in Red Bank and another down in Toms River. Now we were all that was left in the region, plodding through each day without the rush of adrenaline that comes hand-in-hand with the fear of getting beat. I continued, caught up in Haines's rush.

Lindbergh's fame made the case crazy. Every hustler and nut came out of the woodwork offering help—from Al Capone to a boardwalk gypsy named Mother Angeline—and each time I got the story exclusively, courtesy of Henning. Even the cops got

*caught up in the craziness—celebrity over sanity—and the inves-
tigation suffered.*

*For instance, on the very first day, Lindbergh told
Schwarzkopf not to bother the domestic help. "Don't grill them,"
Lindbergh said, "I trust them implicitly." He didn't want to hear
about their potential complicity. He was blinded by his own ego,
fed by his fame. He refused to believe his faithful servants could
be capable of any malevolence toward him because of who he was,
as if his celebrity would inspire their loyalty.*

Schwarzkopf couldn't believe his ears.

*"Colonel," Schwarzkopf pleaded, "these were the last people to
see the baby alive—and the only ones who knew the family's every
move in the days leading up to the kidnapping."*

*Lindbergh wouldn't hear of it, and Schwarzkopf relented. I got
the story, exclusive. The next day's* Mirror *pronounced: LIND-
BERGH: THE BUTLERS DIDN'T DO IT.*

*Schwarzkopf eventually got fed up with Lindbergh's edicts and
had his men interview the baby's nurse, the young and pretty
Betty Gow. Miss Gow, it seems, had a new suitor named Red
Johnson, a Newport yacht crewman by summer and a ne'er-do-
well by winter. So here were two people in the employ of the rich
who maybe wanted to create a little nest egg of their own,
Schwarzkopf reasoned. Reasonable enough.*

*Schwarzkopf sicced Lieutenant Art "Buster" Keaton on Miss
Gow. Keaton's nickname was a double entendre. Buster Keaton
was a comic as big as Chaplin in his day, but there was nothing
funny about Detective Art Keaton. He was all-business, a hard-
knuckled interrogator who cracked more than his share of tough
eggs. You needed someone broken, you called Buster.*

*Keaton tore into Gow, making her account for every minute
before the baby got snatched. Over and over. He hammered her*

about Red, asking questions nice girls shouldn't have to listen to, let alone answer.

But Keaton didn't count on her running in tears to Mrs. Lindbergh, who then ran in tears to her husband, who then tore into Schwarzkopf.

"I'm asking you, no, make that ordering you to leave our servants alone," Lindbergh said, up on his high horse.

Later Henning told me Schwarzkopf had it out with Breckinridge.

"We must have access to the servants," Schwarzkopf said.

"The Colonel says no," Breckinridge said. "He means no."

"This is bizarre, bizarre behavior," Schwarzkopf said. "It's as if he's trying to hide something."

Breckinridge got formal and haughty.

"If, sir, you are intimating that Colonel Lindbergh had something to do with the disappearance of his baby, I assure you that is not the case. You sound like a man with no leads and no ideas. Desperate. To impugn the character of Colonel Lindbergh is disgraceful. And I assure you that this kind of wrong-headed thinking will get you removed from this case, if I have to go all the way to J. Edgar Hoover!"

But Breckinridge was wrong. It was Lindbergh who was desperate, giving audience to every low-life, hustler, and scavenger with a "tip" about the baby.

One day a guy named Mickey Rosner showed up at the estate, saying he was an associate of Al Capone's. Rosner said he could find the baby through his underworld connections. Schwarzkopf wanted to show him the door pronto then tail him. Lindbergh, incredibly, believed the guy could help and insisted on giving him $2,500 in expense money and a copy of the ransom note.

Then along came a southern cop-turned-crook named Gaston Bullock Means, who said he knew the kidnappers and could act as a go-between on the ransom delivery. Schwarzkopf wanted to lock him up and sweat him for a few days, but not Lindbergh. He invited Means into the study, gave him a brandy, and began to help him make the arrangements. Turned out Means was pulling off a first-class swindle of a well-meaning Virginia socialite named Evalyn Walsh McLean, who put up a hundred grand of her husband's hard-earned money to find the baby.

Next up was Al Capone, stewing in an Illinois federal pen. Capone got word to the Lindberghs that if they could secure his release he would help them get the baby back through his connections, which were clearly better than Rosner's. Schwarzkopf tried to put the kibosh on that, saying they were already paying one gangster. Lindbergh passed word that he would make the final decision, not Schwarzkopf.

It was a crazy case and, thanks to Henning, I kept breaking these crazy stories. It got to the point where some other news guys, jealous they were, accused me of making it all up. I said, "Not this time, boys. Even I couldn't make this stuff up."

Meanwhile, Schwarzkopf knew he was losing control of the investigation. Time was going by, March was turning into April. The servants, if involved, had plenty of time to cover their tracks, and Rosner had probably circulated the ransom letter with its secret marks to a few con men, all now in a position to come forward with "inside information" to fleece the Lindberghs.

One day in mid-April, Henning told me Schwarzkopf had gathered his troops and told them forward-march as if the baby were dead.

"Let Lindbergh and Breckinridge get played for chumps," Schwarzkopf said. "We're not playing footsie with any more crooks. Anybody who says they've made contact with the kidnappers, we sweat 'em, we tail 'em, we rubberhose 'em, we do whatever it takes to break this case. Act like there is no more baby to

protect. And, most important, we don't breathe a word of this out of this room. Especially not to Lindbergh and Breckinridge."

Twenty minutes after the meeting, I saw Henning milling around the estate. I flipped him a cigarette.

"What's new?" I asked.

"The chief thinks the baby is dead," Henning said. "Says anybody who thinks otherwise is delusional."

Up till now, the nation was holding out hope, looking in every railroad and bus station, in every abandoned farmhouse, and in every flop hotel for Little Lucky. Now I had a top cop saying he thought the baby was dead. What a story!

I knew it would be better if I got it right from the Schwarz's mouth, so I went looking and found him in the communications garage. I was nervous because Schwarzkopf wasn't the most approachable guy, but I pulled myself up and went right at him.

"Colonel Schwarzkopf," I said, "is it true you think the baby is dead?"

He gave me the same daggers I'd seen him use on Henning.

"Who the hell do you think you are?" he said, crossing his arms like the schoolyard bully. "Get the hell away from me before I lock you up for trespassing."

I beat it and wrote the story anyway, using the old standby: "according to reliable sources close to the investigation."

For the first few weeks I had non-stop exclusives as Henning provided one inside scoop after another. My "trespassing," as Schwarzkopf called it, had paid off big. Each night before I phoned into the office, I made a last trip around the house, shooting the breeze with cops I'd gotten to know a little—all of us keeping an eye out for Schwarzkopf. Then I'd slip off and spy in the windows, to see what high-level skull sessions were going on. I'd see Schwarzkopf huddled with—or arguing with—Breckinridge, or having strategy meetings with his top men—Captain John

Lamb, Buster Keaton, and Detective Nuncio De Gaetano. Even though it was a raw spring and blustery, they almost always cracked a window to let the cigarette and cigar smoke out. I usually spent a half-hour crouched down, shivering under the sill, one ear toward the open window, eavesdropping on all the day's inside business.

Every now and then, Lindbergh would come into the room, and when he did, they all tiptoed around him like he was some crazy Roman emperor.

Schwarzkopf knew Lindbergh was fouling up the investigation and started plotting ways to get rid of him. I heard him ask Breckinridge to pack the Lindberghs up and take them back to Englewood, to the estate of Mrs. Lindbergh's father, Dwight Morrow. I heard him tell Breckinridge they couldn't run an investigation with Lindbergh making side deals with anybody and everybody who claimed to be in touch with the kidnappers.

"He's like the gullible farmer's daughter being wooed by some greaseball Fuller Brush man," I heard Schwarzkopf tell Breckinridge one night. "How can I run an investigation if he's telling every guinea or Jew gangster that comes along he's willing to pay the ransom?!"

"He's trying to protect his baby!" Breckinridge shouted.

"There is no baby, Henry," Schwarzkopf said. "I know nobody wants to hear that, but it's been over three weeks now. We have experience with these things."

The case got more bizarre when a retired grammar school principal named John Condon got involved. Condon was a straight-laced, dogooder geezer right out of King Arthur. A man of honor and integrity, he told us all.

This Condon wrote an open letter to the kidnappers in a Bronx newspaper, offering $1,000 of his own money to sweeten the ransom pie. Two days later he received a letter with strange markings *along the bottom. Condon called the estate and told Lindbergh's secretary he'd made contact with the kidnappers. Believe it or not, the secretary put Lindbergh on the phone. They were so desperate to find that baby alive.*

Condon described the letter he got like a schoolteacher would—the bad English, the misspellings—then told Lindbergh about the weird symbols. Lindbergh was convinced it came from whoever left the original ransom note and invited Condon to come to the estate immediately. Without telling the police, he authorized Condon to be his go-between. Condon began communicating with the kidnappers through ads in the Bronx paper. After a week of messages, the money was readied, and a meeting was arranged in Woodlawn Cemetery in the Bronx.

It was only then that Lindbergh told Schwarzkopf about Condon. Schwarzkopf wanted him tailed. Lindbergh said no. Schwarzkopf wanted to put a few men in the area. Lindbergh said no. Schwarzkopf wanted one of his men to be disguised as a cemetery caretaker. Lindbergh said no. Schwarzkopf gave up and promised to stay away from the ransom exchange. Maybe, if they had swarmed the way Schwarzkopf wanted, they would have caught Bruno Richard Hauptmann that night.

Condon and Lindbergh made the late night delivery of the ransom to a man named "John" in the cemetery. "John" told them the baby was on the boat Nelly *docked off Martha's Vineyard. The next day, Lindbergh flew all over Buzzard's Bay and Vineyard Sound looking for the boat. Nothing.*

Henning gave me the details and I broke the story: HEART-BROKEN LINDY DOUBLE-CROSSED BY 'NAPPERS. Wrote a great snappy lead, too: "The money was delivered, but not the baby." Short and sweet. Said it all.

At this point, I found Haines's account rich in details, but short on humanity. At times, it crossed into smug and self-serving. It was about how he covered the story, how he won the game. And there was a cruelty to it, especially in the way he portrayed Lindbergh— sometimes as the strong-jawed hero, other times as naïve and egocentric. There seemed to be no in-between.

I took this up with Haines the next morning, after we settled in for coffee in the Oceanview's dining room. I expected him to dismiss me as soft.

"It all goes back to my earlier point," he said. "Lindbergh's celebrity overpowered everything, even the fact he was human. He wasn't a real, flesh-and-blood person to me at this point. He was perfect fodder for newspaper stories, that's all. Any compassion I should have felt for him—and I admit this was wrong—was lost in the chase."

"But what about Mrs. Lindbergh?" I asked. "She obviously moved you."

Haines squirmed in his chair and looked out the window to the pond where a flock of seagulls were picking at something on the ground.

"I trampled her in the chase, too," he said with an exhale. "I've lived with that, but what I did was deplorable. Especially considering I saw her grief with my own two eyes. Unforgivable, because I knew she was pretty much going it alone."

He paused and gathered his breath.

"From my nightly eavesdropping trips I discovered the Lindberghs had a scheduled appointment every night in the breakfast nook to discuss the day's developments. And that's exactly what it was like most nights. Like a press briefing, for chrissakes! She would ask questions and he would answer—short and stiff, to the point, as if he were talking to some functionary like Schwarzkopf, not the woman who was the baby's *mother.* She would beg him for details, and he would become detached, withdrawn ... cold, even. I could see how much that upset her. There were times when he would touch her, try to comfort her, but you could tell intimacy didn't come easy for him. I guess he was more comfortable alone in the clouds. When he left, she would cry, just like the first night I'd spied on her. Inside, I was crying with her. I wanted to reach through the glass and curtains and caress and comfort her."

Haines looked at me, perhaps to see my reaction to this gentler side of him. I nodded, a sign of approval, and he continued.

"Night after night, I watched Lindbergh move from room to room in his gray suit. It was like watching the same stilted silent film over and over through the lacy curtains. Every night, it was the same. The husband, stoic, businesslike, detached; his wife, tearful, broken, and left to fend for herself.

"I always wondered why and when Lindbergh became so aloof. And whose fault was it, really? Was it when he was flying over the empty, black expanse of the Atlantic, more alone than any man in history who ever lived to tell about it? When he was flying so low through mist and sea spray that he was no more than an engine sputter or lapse into sleep from being swallowed by God's great ocean? Being that close to death for so long, knowing you will die alone and never be found, can leave a man broken in places most of us don't know we have.

"Or was it after he touched down at Le Bourget, when the world embraced him with such suffocating might that it squeezed whatever was left of the private Charles Lindbergh out of the public Lucky Lindy, making the loner run and cower deep inside the hero?

"Did his celebrity alienate him from the rest of us? Did it make him distrust the motives of all those who wanted to touch him, befriend him, or love him? Or was he just born like that? I don't know. Maybe he found it easier to be detached, and alone. Sometimes it is truly easier that way."

Haines said all this like a man with experience in such loneliness. I wanted to ask him about it, but he kept talking.

"All I know is that I never saw Charles Lindbergh shed one tear or show an ounce of emotion through the whole ordeal, except on the day they found Little Lucky. I'll never forget that day. It was May 12, 1932, 72 days after the disappearance."

7

"There are two kinds of Mays in Jersey," Haines said. "One of blossoms and glowing sunshine, of clear skies and promise of summer; and one of damp, dismal drizzle, of winter's final sniffles like a cold you can't shake. That May, the May of 1932, was like the second. Chilly and wet, March in disguise."

Haines closed the robe tight around his neck and shivered slightly as he said this, as if the ancient chill was with him still.

"Mid-afternoon on May 12, one of these rainy days, two lumber truckers pulled off Mount Rose Hill Road just outside Hopewell to relieve themselves. They walked about 75 feet into the woods, where one of them, a black fellow named William Allen, came upon a mess he first thought was a rotting pile of deer entrails and organs, the remains of a hunter's field dressing. Then he saw a tiny foot sticking out of the leaves. Then things came into a head-spinning, grisly focus. A skull, still partially covered with patches of matted blond hair. A face, blackened by decomposition, but with the soft, angelic features of a child somewhat intact.

"Allen screamed for his partner, Orville Wilson. Wilson stumbled through the brush, still buttoning up, thinking maybe ol' Willy got his foot caught in a raccoon trap. When he found Willy and saw what he saw, they both stood there stammering until Willy staggered off and threw up."

Haines stopped here and clutched the robe tighter, and his body produced one wracked shiver.

The body was not a pretty sight, he said. Both hands, one leg, and his belly had been gnawed away by animals, and his skin was withered and leathery. The body had been carelessly buried, then covered with leaves by somebody in a hurry. The two truck drivers knew exactly what they where looking at: the corpse of Charles Lindbergh Jr.

"Little Unlucky," Haines said.

The men ran back to their truck and backtracked to Hopewell and stopped when they saw a police car outside the barbershop. Inside, a local cop was getting a shave.

"'Willy found the baby!' Orville yelled.

"The cop jumped up so quick he's lucky he didn't end up with his throat slit."

Haines was at the estate when he saw two carloads of detectives speed off.

"I found Henning, ricky-tick. 'What's going on?' I asked.

"'They found the baby,' he said.

"'Dead?' I asked.

"'Dead,' he answered.

"'Where?' I asked.

"'In the woods,' said Henning. "Four miles from here. Mount Rose. I can't talk now.'

"I got in one more question. 'How long do they think he's been dead?'

"'From the start. I gotta go,' he said.

"Henning, too, was headed for the woods, and he ordered me to stay away. 'This is too hot right now,' he said. 'Meet me later at the coffee shop and I'll give you the details.'"

Haines stayed at the estate and watched as Schwarzkopf went into the house, presumably to give Mrs. Lindbergh the news.

"He came out a few minutes later, his eyes moist, but still with that hard-ass soldier's look on his face."

Colonel Lindbergh was out on another ransom scam, this one down in Cape May, New Jersey. A shipping magnate named John

Hughes Curtis had convinced him the kidnappers would be waiting there to complete a baby-for-cash exchange. Lindbergh was on a yacht with a satchel of money waiting for the weather to clear for the off-shore swap. Then came the telegram, and he was raced back to Hopewell with a state police escort of motorcycles and patrol cars.

Haines phoned in the baby's death and the *Mirror* printed an exclusive, a story with a massive two-word headline on the front page.

"Two words: BABY DEAD. Said it all, but the story was short on details," Haines said. "I caught up with Henning at about six in town. While locals dined on meatloaf and pie *à la mode* and shook their heads over the terrible news, Henning hunched over our table with his shoulders squared like a fullback and laid out all the facts for me."

Haines was told how the truckers found the body, how the body was positioned, how the baby was still dressed in the flannel night shirt hand-made by nurse Betty Gow. Henning gave him details about other evidence at the scene, like the discarded burlap bag the kidnappers had carried the body in.

"He told me the cops figured the baby was killed—either on purpose or accidentally—the very night of the kidnapping. He told me the cause of death was a skull fracture. Then he told me about the condition of the body.

"'I've seen a lot of bad stuff,' Henning said. 'But this was the worst. There were hardened cops puking. I told them, *Get hold of yourselves, for God sakes!*'"

Haines said he turned a little green himself when Henning described the baby's skin as looking like "a catcher's mitt left outside over the winter."

"I used those exact words in the paper," Haines said. "Then you know what the son-of-a-bitch said to me? He says, 'Hey, Haines, you want a piece of pie or something?' That gave him a big laugh. But then he got dead serious, looked over both shoulders and leaned in close to me.

"'They're bringing the body down to the Swayze Funeral Parlor, 415 Greenwood Avenue, Trenton,' he tells me. 'Walt Swayze is county coroner, too, which I guess is good for business if you're him. They're bringing in Nurse Betty to ID the body. When that's done, Schwarzkopf is going to hold a press conference in a couple of hours back at the estate, giving all the details. Well, almost all the details.'

"'What does that mean?' I asked.

"'That means the chief doesn't want to disclose the condition of the baby's body,' Henning whispered. 'Colonel Lindbergh and him decided to keep it from the Missus, because they don't want to upset her any more than she already is. What that means to you is this: Don't write anything about how the baby looked.'"

Here Haines paused.

"I knew it was the right thing to do, but I went on the offensive, playing the newspaper tough-guy.

"'What does she think, he's all pretty and clean and freshly powdered after being left out in the woods for six weeks?' I asked.

"'It doesn't matter what she thinks,' Henning said. 'What matters is the chief and Colonel Lindbergh don't want her thinking too much about it. That's the point.'"

Haines stopped and looked at me. "You're a newspaperman. Do you think that was a reasonable request?"

It was the first time in our conversations that he'd asked me for an opinion. I was surprised and somewhat honored.

"Yes, I do. Henning gave you the critical information: The baby was dead, you knew the cause of death, and you had the police theory that the baby was killed the night of the kidnapping. The gory details about the body seem irrelevant and printing them would border on salacious. It's self-serving and gives the illusion of important information. Like you said, a body left outside for six weeks isn't a pretty sight, but people can use their imaginations, those who want to. Those who don't, why jam it down their throats?"

"Because it's not about information. It's about competition! Don't you get that by now?" he said. He leaned up in his chair and waved one bony finger above his head. "Right or wrong, I had to beat those news bums sitting on their asses drinking coffee at the depot—whatever the cost. I wanted to win! Looking back, I should have been happy with my winning run of exclusives and played this one for the tie. But I wanted to keep winning and—just like a gambler who plays till he loses—I kept pressing."

He studied my face then, and, for the first time in our conversation, I started to understand why Fred Haines was telling me all this. It was a confession of his own.

"I disgust you, don't I?"

"No, you don't. I'm a newspaperman. I understand. I don't agree, but I understand."

Haines accepted that and continued his story.

"So I said to Henning, 'You're putting me in a tough spot, here. You give me all these details, tell me the rest of the press will never know, then tell me not to write it. I'm watching my exclusive go poof! I think I got to write it.'

"'And I think you don't. Lookit, Haines, I've done you a lot of favors,' Henning reminded me. 'Now I'm asking you for one. One lousy favor. Keep this out of the papers.'

"'I don't know if I can do that,' I responded.

"'You will,' he said.

"All I said was 'I can't promise.'

"'You have to,' said Henning.

"'But it's news,' I said.

"'It's only news if you blab it,' Henning said."

***

"He had you there," I said to Haines.

"I guess he did. It was an excellent point. I just didn't realize it at the time. Then Henning said to me, 'Don't you care anything about this woman's feelings? She's been through hell—now you're gonna add to it?'

"Right there, I had my out. I should have let that sink in a little and backed off. Instead, I got up on my high horse.

"'Not as much as I care about informing the public,' I responded.

"'Baloney,' Henning said. 'You don't care about that, you only care about the glory these stories bring you.'

"He was right about that, of course, but I kept trying to take the high road. I spewed about the public's right to know and revealing the unvarnished truth to the reader. All the high-minded journalistic-ese I could muster. Truth was, I wanted to beat the other reporters and Henning knew it.

"Finally, Henning had enough. 'Cut the crap, Haines,' he said. 'You work for the *Daily Mirror*, for chrissakes!'"

"He had you there, too," I said to Haines.

"He sure did," Haines said.

Haines said he made a deal with Henning.

"I told him I wouldn't write the details unless I got them official, from the coroner or Schwarzkopf or Lindbergh himself."

"Henning said, 'How will I know you just didn't pretend you got them official?'

"'C'mon, Henning, you can trust me,' I said.

"'No, I can't. Hell no, Haines. Not on this one,' Henning said.

"He had me there, too," said Haines.

***

Haines said he knew he would never get it "official." Betty Gow was under protection, with Detective De Gaetano all but hand-cuffed to her. The truckers were told if they talked, they'd get locked up as suspected accomplices. Swayze, the coroner, knew he'd quickly become the *former* coroner if he talked.

Henning went back to the estate to get ready for the news con-ference, and Haines called his editor, Dicks.

"I made a big mistake. I told him I was holding a couple of aces. I knew where the body was and what condition it was in. And of all the reporters, only I knew.

"Henning was dead-on about me. My ego overrode my com-mon sense. I was a blood-and-guts tabloid guy. I was conditioned that way. I wanted something more."

Haines said he decided to "pull a page out of my old Ruth Snyder book" and was determined to get exclusive pictures of the baby's tiny coffin at the funeral home.

"What could it hurt? I thought."

Now he handed me his manuscript again. "Find the part about the photograph."

I went through the papers and came upon a subhead: *Little Unlucky.*

I found the Mirror *photographer, a young, hulking boozer named Max Jacobs, down at press headquarters in the train depot, killing time with other photogs. Official word of the body discovery was still a few hours from hitting the street, so I gave Max the old high sign.*

"Maxie, let's go, we got a job," I whispered.

"What?" he said, too loud.

"C'mon, let's git," I whispered again. "It's big. Bigger than big. Let's go make some news."

Max liked that. He was an aggressive young bull, built like a leather-neck football lineman, the kind of photog who didn't mind getting thrown out of places or engaging in a little fisticuffs with the NYPD back home.

We loaded his gear into Uncle Chuck's car, and I filled him in as we headed down the Lincoln Highway to Trenton.

Swayze's was right off Highway 1, about three blocks from the Jersey statehouse. It was dusk then, and the funeral home was dark and ghostly, except for some light coming out of the basement windows. The only sign of life was a trooper standing guard out front, there to protect the evidence. He looked bored and half-asleep on his feet. I drove down a side street and killed the headlights. Around back was the casket dock, and I parked between a black Caddy hearse and flower car.

We jumped up on the dock and the freight elevator was right there, the doors wide open, inviting us in. We stepped into the mouth of this forbidden cave.

"Up or down?" Max asked.

"What the hell, down," I said.

I pulled the heavy steel doors with a canvas strap and was relieved to find they were well-oiled and closed with a gentle click. The elevator was quiet, too. The electric motor hummed no louder than a purr. On cat's feet, me and Max started nosing around. We got to a dimly lit room, where we could make out refrigerated morgue lockers in the shadows. Max flipped on a light switch.

The fluorescent bulbs flickered and flashed, like lightning in a laboratory scene from a Bela Lugosi movie. In these flashes, I saw a room lined with stainless steel cabinets. In the middle of the floor, directly under a round, low-hanging spotlight, was a large stainless steel table with a splashboard and gutter that went into the floor. The last brilliant flash of light revealed a small mound covered by a blue rubber sheet on top of the table.

"Eureka! Jackpot, baby!" Max shouted in a loud whisper.

I started to feel sick.

"Come to papa!" Max said as he walked toward the table, jamming the film plate into his Speed Graphic camera like a soldier bangs a bullet clip into a gun.

He grabbed the rubber sheet with one hand and looked back at me.

"You ready?"

"Jesus Christ" was all I could say.

He pulled back the sheet and there was Little Lucky. Little Unlucky, now Little Ugly. That's what he looked like. An ugly doll. A weather-beaten, life-size lost doll you found discarded on a riverbank or on a railroad track or floating in a pond or tar pit. It was all that Henning described, but worse. My eyes took it all in before I could turn away. I lost my breath, but not before the stench hit me. As I write this, I can still smell it.

Max didn't miss a beat. The flash popped and lit the room, and I could hear him changing one film plate after another. Bang, pop, rip, bang, pop, rip, bang, pop, rip.

As soon as I could breathe, I said, "Okay, Maxie, let's get the hell out of here."

"A few more, Haines-boy, just a few more," he said, again too loud. I couldn't believe his calm. "Just a few more."

"Jesus, Maxie, how can you stand it?" I cried in a whisper.

"Just another stiff when you look through the lens, my friend," he said, cool as a surgeon. "Seen one, you seen 'em all. Trick is, you don't look at the faces."

I was sweating and trying not to breathe. I started to feel light-headed, but I held on. I knew if I fainted, Max would have a story to bust my nuts with for all time.

"Maxie, now, let's go."

I knew what getting caught meant. It meant Schwarzkopf charging us with everything but murdering the baby, from trespassing to tampering with evidence.

"Maxie, let's go before we end up in the clink ... or worse."

The Jersey state troopers, even in those days, were a tough bunch. They had a reputation for back-room rough stuff.

"Okay. Vamoose!" he said, re-covering what was left of Little Unlucky with the rubber sheet.

We ran down the hall and jumped back into the freight elevator, this time slamming the door.

Neither of us said a word as the elevator hummed up.

We knew what we had.

As we hurried across the parking lot, we got caught in the headlights of an official-looking black sedan.

"You, two! Hold it right there!"

The man behind the wheel had a big, official-sounding voice. But when he got out of the car, I wondered how such a scrawny body could hold such a voice. The man was near 70, with gray hair and a pencil mustache. He wore a baggy black suit that fluttered in the wind. No doubt it was Swayze, the dignified-looking county coroner. His eyes went right away to Max's camera, and he suddenly got the whole picture.

"You newspaper bastards! Is nothing sacred to you?" he screamed. His voice bounced around the parking lot like a baritone billiard ball.

"Take it easy, Pops," Max said. "We just got here."

"Gimme that. Gimme that goddamn camera." The old guy lunged at Max.

"Not on your life, Pops," Max said and gave the old coroner a Bronko Nagurski straight arm that knocked his spectacles off as we made a run for the car.

"I'll have you arrested! You bastards! I'm the county coroner! This is my responsibility!" he screamed. "Police! Help! Police!"

He flailed at Uncle Chuck's car as we piled in, then grabbed hold of the driver's side door. I tried to close it, but the old guy was strong. We used the car door as a rope in a tug of war for a few seconds, then finally I got out, pried his hands off the handle—it wasn't easy—and shoved him hard. He was gasping and staggered back on spaghetti legs and, just like that, all the fight drained out of him. He stood there looking small and scared.

Then suddenly I remembered why I came in the first place: to get the baby's condition all official.

"Mr. Swayze," I asked, "is it true the baby's hands and legs were gnawed away by wild animals?"

"POLICE!" he yelled. His voice climbed high like a frightened woman's.

Just then I heard Max say, "Haines, front and center, babe ..." The trooper from out front was double-timing it around the side of the building, hand undoing the flap on his holster. "Let's skedaddle. Let's go!" Max said.

I dove into the car and hit the gas hard. Now it was Uncle Chuck's Lucky 6 versus the trooper's Colt six. The trooper yelled, "HOLD IT!" and then came the crack of gunfire. I figured the first was in the air; the next was coming through the back window. My neck suddenly felt cold and exposed. I slumped down and swerved to give the trooper a moving target.

"Hang on, Maxie!"

"Keep it going, Haines-boy! Keep it going!" Max whooped like a kid on a rollercoaster.

I heard a second crack as we turned a corner hard, and Max yelled, "Straighten her out, Haines!" We passed an on-coming Trenton black-and-white, and I saw red siren lights start up in my rearview mirror. I took the first turn, then the next, then the next, through the compact neighborhoods of downtown Trenton. Five or six side streets later, I was convinced we shook 'em, and me and Max started breathing easier. I stayed off Highway 1, trying to find my way back to Hopewell on back roads.

Haines interrupted me and asked me where I was in the manuscript.

"Stop reading there," he said, once I told him, "because I have to explain what happened next."

"Me and Max were both quiet for awhile. Finally Max said, 'This is too hot to trust to a courier,' as he patted the film plates. 'Let me borrow the car and take it to New York myself.'

"I said, 'Hold on, Maxie, let's think this through.'

"He said, 'Nothing to think about Haines, brother. We got the exclu of a lifetime.'

"I reminded him of my deal with Henning. And about Schwarzkopf. And Lindbergh. And poor Mrs. Lindbergh!

"'We print these photos and our names will be mud down here,' I said. 'This is bad stuff we got here.'

"'Better to be mud, than to be broke, brother,' Max said. 'If the bosses find out we got these and didn't print them, we'll both be out on our ass.'

"'How will they know?' I asked.

"'No offense, brother, but two can keep a secret if one is dead,' Max responded. 'B'sides, for all we know, the cops are calling around to papers right now, trying to kill these shots. You told Dicks we were going to the funeral home, right? He'll know it was us. The way I see it, we have no choice.'

"I sat in silence, and my silence was complicit agreement."

***

Haines said this with such sadness that I felt I should commiserate. I reached over and patted his arm, which was resting on a dining hall table, with his hand wrapped around a now-cold cup of coffee.

"Maybe Max was right. You had no choice," I offered.

Haines stiffened in his chair and answered, his voice rising.

"We had no choice? Of course we had a choice! We could have lied and said we never got in the funeral home. We could have lied and said we got in but never found the baby. We could have lied and said we found the baby, but were too sick over the sight to work. We could have 'accidentally' exposed or dropped or lost the film plates. We could have done a million things to not print the picture of that baby. There were a million ways out!

"But we both acted like we had no choice. Our egos—dammit, our own meager *celebrity* got in the way. And it was wrong, it was the wrong thing to do. And believe me, a day doesn't go by that I don't regret it."

"Why does this haunt you so much?" I asked. "It was such a long time ago."

"Because it ruined the one chance I had at a normal life. I didn't know it then, but that picture ... aw, forget it, for now. Keep reading. It won't make any sense, anyways, till you get to the end."

Max dropped me off in Hopewell, and he zoomed up to New York as fast as the Chevy could take him. I caught the tail end of the Schwarzkopf news conference—the cleaned-up, antiseptic version. He gave no details about the body, and he wasn't asked by the hundred or so press bums there. I figured they'd been warned.

I stayed in the shadows waiting for Schwarzkopf. As the other newsmen raced out to call in, I had a shot at Schwarzkopf to myself.

"Sir ... sir ... this is difficult," I stammered. "But can you say anything about the condition of the baby's body?"

His expression was impossible to mimic—something between alarm and disgust.

"No, I can't. And I won't," he said. "Now, once and for all, you get the hell away from me and stay the hell away from me."

"Colonel," I said, in a very confidential whisper made raspy by my dry throat. "Is it true that parts of the baby were ravaged by wild animals?"

Schwarzkopf wheeled around and yanked me by the lapels. For the second time that night, I was surprised by another man's strength. He shook me like a child's rattle and screamed into my face.

"Wild animals? You're an animal for asking a question like that, you sonofabitch. Don't you have a single ounce of decency? This is a baby ... a little baby ... with a mother!"

"I'll never forget that," Haines interrupted. "I felt his hot breath and spit on my face, and his eyes got squinty with a hatred that scared me enough to make me piss my pants a little. I never told anybody that before.

A trooper pried his way in between Haines and Schwarzkopf.

"'Easy, Chief,' he said. 'This bum's not worth it.'"

Haines shook his head. "A bum! Can you imagine? That's what I became to these guys," he said. "Maybe they were right. Go on, keep reading."

Schwarzkopf flung me back with a strong-arm shove, and I stumbled and fell. He was surrounded by at least twenty bluecoat troopers, but no one tried to break my fall. I saw Henning off to the side. He looked like he wanted to kill me, too. Schwarzkopf straightened himself and brushed down his jacket, as if he were trying to wipe off my germs.

"To answer your question, the baby was not 'ravaged by wild animals' as you suggest," he said, a lid now on his boiling anger. "And you ask me or anybody else again, I'll have you locked up for obstruction of justice, evidence tampering, public drunkenness, and whatever else I can make stick. Got it?"

He stormed out with his cadre of cops, and I staggered off to call Dicks. I knew if we published those photos, there would be more than all hell to pay, so I hoped to talk Dicks out of it. I rehearsed the arguments over and over in my head.

It was immoral. It was invasive. Mrs. Lindbergh. The memory of the baby. It was just plain bad. Wrong.

I was wandering around the estate, dazed really, trying to fig-
ure out what to do, when Lindbergh arrived with full police
escort. I stood near the entrance as he pulled himself out of the
car, slow and stiff. He looked tired and hollow in his three-piece
gray suit, like a dressed-up invalid.

Now I had a chance to ask him about the baby's condition. I
tried to talk myself into it. Why? I don't know. I was hoping if he
told me—and I had it in his words—it would make it easier to
convince Dicks not to print the photos. I repeated over and over in
my head, "a victim is merely a character in a newspaper story."
But as I moved closer to Lindbergh, I couldn't muster the courage,
or maybe find the lack of decency in myself, to ask. He passed me,
and I could see his eyes wet with tears, tired and red from the
ordeal. He passed within a yard of me. I remember thinking, at
that moment, if I had no idea who this man was, if I had just
spotted him, a stranger in a Midtown crowd of strangers on any
ordinary day, I would have known by the look on his face that
this man just lost a child.

"Colonel Lindbergh ..."

He turned in my direction and looked at me with those terribly
sad and tired eyes.

"I'm sorry," was all I could say.

That chapter of the manuscript ended there.

"It makes me sound like a decent guy, doesn't it?" Haines asked.

"It makes it sound like you have a conscience, anyway," I said.

"Well, here's the part I didn't write.

"When I called Dicks with my story, I knew Max had already
delivered the photos. I was hoping to engage Dicks in some ethical
give-and-take about the rights and wrongs of putting a dead baby

on the cover of the *Daily Mirror* for all the world to see. I never got a word in edgewise."

"'Jesus Christ! You boys did great!' Dicks shouted into the phone before I could even finish saying hello. 'We're gonna sell 2 million copies! Mr. Hearst was already on the line saying this picture was going to make this newspaper profitable for the next two years, at least!'

"I felt nauseous. I had a deal with Henning, and I still didn't have the details confirmed—even though I saw them up close, confirmed in their most horrible form. And we had the pictures.

"But the pictures didn't tell the whole story. They didn't tell the story of the frustration and anger busting out of Schwarzkopf, or the pain on Lindbergh's face. They didn't tell the story of Mrs. Lindbergh about to be haunted for life with a horrible photographic image of what was left of *her* baby.

"Oh, I felt so sick! I wished Henning had never told me about the baby's condition, I wished I never made any deal with him, and I wished to hell we hadn't gotten those pictures. Now Dicks wanted the words to match. 'Maxie told me something about animals. Tell me about the animals.'

"I tried to steer him in a different direction. 'The story here, Dicks, is the atrocity committed by human animals, criminal animals, that could kill and discard a child like this. My story isn't about the body. It should be one of outrage, of screaming bloody murder, of calling for the eyes and ears of the people who did this—'

"Dicks interrupted me, saying, 'You mean the people who left a dead or defenseless baby in the woods to be picked clean by forest creatures. See, Haines, the details about the body are crucial, absolutely crucial, to your story. Give me the details, goddamn it, or it's your ass!'

"I knew then it was a lost cause.

"'What Maxie told you is true,' I said, and hung up."

The next day's *Mirror* carried another screaming headline, LITTLE UNLUCKY!, with an underline that said, *LINDBERGH BABY MAULED IN WOODS*. Underneath the headlines was a gruesome picture of the baby on the mortuary slab. Inside was the full story under the byline Frederick G. Haines.

***

It was the one newspaper clip Haines did not keep.

"It's burned into my brain enough as it is. And just when I thought it couldn't get worse, it did."

An engraver and pressman at the *Mirror* ran off a few hundred prints of the photo to sell. By nine the next morning, they were in Trenton outside Swayze Funeral Parlor, where a throng had gathered, selling Little Unlucky's picture for five bucks apiece. Back in Hopewell, the *Mirror* tripled its delivery to the press headquarters at the train depot. Another twenty bundles were distributed around town, and two were dropped off in the driveway leading to the Lindbergh estate.

"When I showed my face at the depot the next morning, I got the cold shoulder. I was the pariah of the national press corps," Haines said. "To be the pariah of all the parasites feeding off Lindbergh's grief, well, you can't go much lower than that."

A *New York Times* reporter broke the silence.

"I don't see you gloating today, Haines!" he said. "What's the matter? Conscience got your tongue?"

"Just doing my job," Haines replied, weakly.

"If that's the job, God help us all."

***

Later, Haines drove up the mountain to the Lindbergh estate.

"I had to face the music from Henning. I owed him that. He found me within minutes.

"'Hey, Haines! I got a scoop for you,' he said with a sharp, angry whisper. He grabbed me by the elbow and led me around back of the garage by the garbage cans. He spun me toward him and caught me clean with a shot to the solar plexus. I doubled over, gasping for air.

"'Hey! You hear the news?' he hissed. I knew what was coming. A left hook to the ear, which rang like a dog-whistle through my head and drove me to one knee. Then came the right uppercut, which, luckily for me, landed square on my forehead instead of my mouth or nose. I heard Henning's knuckles crack, and I fell back, ass end into a muddy puddle.

"Henning stood over me, breathing hard and rubbing his hand. He was getting ready for Round 2.

"I sat in the mud and held up my hands.

"'Look, Henning, no hard feelings,' I said. 'I know I deserve this.'

"He grabbed me by the lapels and pulled me up.

"'No, Haines,' he spat through gritted teeth. 'What you deserve is for me to pull out my snubnose and put a slug through that stupid excuse of a brain. What you deserve is me throwing your carcass on the trash heap with the rest of the garbage. That's what you deserve. That's what I wish I could give you!'

"Then he threw me down again.

"That was the beginning of the end. Henning ditched me, and no other cop would be caught dead talking to me. Schwarzkopf sent word I would be arrested on the spot if I went back to the estate. I fell back with the pack, the biggest bum of the news bums.

"A few days later Dicks called and said, 'Now that the baby's been found, this case is really going to heat up. Winchell wants to go on the case full-time.' Dicks then spelled it out for me: My job was to be Winchell's caddie, to supply information and quotes and leave all the writing to him. If I had any guts, I would have quit on the spot and headed back to New York, but I had another reason to stay in Hopewell …

"… and she was the other reason the Lindbergh baby pictures would haunt me the rest of my life."

8

"Who is *she*?" I asked. "Mrs. Lindbergh?"

Haines had delivered the line with such regret and self-inflicted despair, I knew love was involved. Had the aviator's wife become the object of his affection? Crazier things have happened. There's a saying among reporters when a preposterous news story hits: "You can't make this stuff up."

"What?" Haines snapped out of his depressive trance. "Mrs. Lindbergh! Are you nuts?"

Haines wanted to return to his room. When I got behind the chair to push, he waved me off.

"I got it."

It was a slow journey. He pushed hard on the rubberized wheels to get started, then stopped frequently to rub his sore hands. We were alone in the long hallway, and the overhead fluorescent lights reflected off the linoleum floor like street lamps on a frozen pond. The lonely, stark scene made me think of a dead man's walk to the electric chair. At that very moment, Haines said, "Why do I feel like Ruth Snyder?"

***

Back in his room, Haines pulled out a large envelope from beneath the folders of news clips and handed it to me.

"Open that up. And be careful."

Inside was an obituary, brittle with spotty water marks and worn from overhandling, making it look much older than it actually was.

"Be careful, now. That one will break and scatter like sand in the wind."

Sara (Lawson) Frelinger, 88, of Hopewell, chairwoman of several charities

Sara Frelinger, a lifelong Hopewell resident who was known for her charitable work in the community and the county, died peacefully at home yesterday morning surrounded by her children.

Mrs. Frelinger was predeceased by her husband of 57 years, James Frelinger, who took over his father's drug store in Hopewell in the 1930s and built a successful chain of 10 pharmacies throughout central New Jersey. The couple was active in several local organizations and charities including the Mercer County Association for the Mentally Retarded and the Central Jersey Food Bank, both of which Mrs. Frelinger served as chairwoman. Mr. Frelinger died in 1989.

She was predeceased also by her oldest child, James Jr., who died at age 29 in 1962.

Mrs. Frelinger is survived by her son Richard and his wife, Sheryl, of Princeton Township, daughter Caroline Tuft and her husband, David, of Lambertville, and daughter Susan Stewart and her husband, Alfred, of Worcester, Massachusetts, and seven grandchildren.

There was more. A few warm comments from people who knew of her dedicated charitable work, a listing of the organizations she was involved with, and details of the funeral arrangements.

The date on the obituary was August 15, 1991.

Haines had his eyes closed as I read, rolling his chair forward a few inches and then back again, a wheelchair-bound man's equivalent of pacing.

When I was done, he began.

"Every story is a house of mirrors. Look one way, you see things from one angle. Look another way, there's a different angle. And on and on. Infinite angles make the complete picture. Most times, we look just one way and think we know the truth. But when you look at my face, you can't see what's in the back of my mind."

"Of course," I said. "But if a house of mirrors creates infinite images and angles, we can never know a complete story, or the truth in it, because the reflected images never end."

"Easy, kiddo, don't hurt your head!" he exclaimed. "I'm talking about the truth of motivation. In my case, to understand why I never revealed Bruno's confession, you have to know who *she* is. Because without *her,* you can't get the whole picture."

I carefully laid the obituary on his bedspread, and his magnified eyes followed. "Yes, that's right. Handle her gently."

***

During the first few days of the Lindbergh case, Haines was living on nothing but coffee, cigarettes, and competitive juice. He was sleeping in the Chevy, taking catnaps on some Sourland Mountain dirt road, using his overcoat for a blanket, and running the motor for heat.

"Looking back, I'm lucky I didn't asphyxiate myself," he said.

He cleaned up in the restroom of the town Esso station.

While caffeine, nicotine, and adrenaline may have been staples of old-time newspapermen, "they can only sustain you so long,"

Haines said. "After a while, I needed a bed, a bath, and a place to call home."

When the news hordes arrived in Hopewell, the rooming houses booked quickly. The *Times* took an entire house for its staff, as did United Press International. Local landlords doubled, then tripled their rates.

"The locals were renting out spare bedrooms, attics, garage lofts," Haines said. "Christ, they would have rented you a pile of hay in a manger to make a side buck.

"Hopewell wasn't much in those days—and probably still isn't today. The main drag was called Broad Street, and there was a general store, a feed store with a porch where locals chaw'ed and jawed, the little coffee shop where I met Henning, and a town hall. It wasn't unusual to see horse-drawn flatbeds driven by farmers clip-clopping in town."

There were a couple of old churches downtown: The Presbyterian was white clapboard; the Baptist made of fieldstone. Around the downtown were maybe eight or nine blocks of tidy neighborhoods, with houses mostly built around the Civil War era. They were sturdy, angular homes—some large, some small, some brick, some wood-sided.

"All in all, it was a modest town; too worn around the edges to be quaint, but not a down-and-out hick town, either," Haines said. "Everybody seemed to know and tolerate one another like good small-town folk do."

After four nights in the car, Haines drove to the neighborhood off Broad Street.

"There were plenty of 'Room to Rent' signs. But I stopped at a house on Second Street—Number 4, it was ... a plain white mill house with a covered front porch. Nothing remarkable, nothing to make me stop, but I did.

"Now what brings a man to one place and not another?" he asked. "How does fate decide when to kiss your lips or kick your ass? Or does fate simply supply the other characters and scenery in the ongoing comedy or tragedy of your life? In other words, is the script the same, no matter where you go, no matter who you meet? If I was destined to fall in love, did it matter that I went to Number 4, Second Street, or would I have met destiny at Number 2, Fourth Street as well? And whose fate was in control, mine or hers? Or did our fates work in concert, conspiring to twist and intertwine our lives to play some cosmic practical joke on both of us?"

He stopped, as if waiting for an answer.

"I don't know," I said finally. "Serendipity?"

"Serendipity? Hah!" he waved his hand dismissively. "A word for dip-shits. A fairy-tale word. A sugar-coated lie! Because serendipity doesn't work alone, my friend. Bitter is never too far behind sweet. The iron fist never concealed too long in the velvet glove. The same gentle hand that caresses your damp chest and soothes your pulsating heart can also plunge in and rip it out."

Haines knocked on the door at 4 Second Street. A large man wearing green work pants with suspenders over a flannel shirt answered. Haines stood there in his charcoal three-piece suit, rumpled from three days of camp in the Chevy, his felt fedora in hand.

"I must've looked like a city slicker who fell off the hobo car of a freight train. When I introduced myself, the man said, 'Oh, you're one of those city newspaper fellas,' and I figured that was that.

"Instead, he gave me a square country handshake and invited me in."

The man had a square country name, Jack Lawson, and he showed Haines the rooms.

"We're not in the boarding house business, but you fellas all need a place to stay, so we made a little apartment out of the upstairs two bedrooms," Lawson told Haines. "It's just me, the wife, and our daughter, so we can squeeze in downstairs."

The rooms were tight. One had a hardwood chair and plain desk, the other a double bed, with no head or foot board. There was a toilet with a tub off the bedroom, and two rules: no smoking and no overnight visitors.

"There's the front porch for smoking," Lawson said. "Overnight visitors you'll have to take somewhere else."

The first thing Haines did was to take a hot bath in the chipped claw-foot tub, then a nap on the spongy mattress, drifting quickly into a deep sleep.

***

Haines took the obituary off the bed and put it in the envelope as carefully as he had taken it out. He wheeled back to his cabinet and traded the obituary for the manuscript. When he found the right spot, he gave me an introduction.

"I didn't spend a lot of time there the first week, only enough to know the Lawsons had clock-like, mechanical routines," he said. "Each morning, I heard an alarm bell right at six, the kettle whistle ten minutes later, then the toilet flush and the bath faucets churn, which made the pipes rattle in the walls. At seven-thirty, as I tried to sleep through this dull racket, I heard the front door close, and light footsteps on the front porch. I admit, those light footsteps got me curious—I knew it wasn't old man Lawson leaving—but not curious enough to hop out of bed on those cold March mornings."

Haines closed his eyes tight, again, his way to black out everything but the grainy mental image buried deep in his memory, like a film archivist rescuing disintegrating celluloid.

"Read it to me," he said, "out loud."

It was one of those very ordinary mornings when I first saw her. I was standing in the front window in only pants and an undershirt, looking at the weather, when I heard the front door open. She emerged from under the porch roof, and I watched her walk away. She was a little taller than the average woman and thinner, too. Her navy wool coat set off her blonde hair, which glistened like gold in the morning sunlight. Later on, I would discover her hair was as light and feathery in texture as it was rich in color. Angelic even. When I held her in my arms, I would caress her hair and twirl it in my fingers. When we were intimate, she would lie with her head on my chest, and her hair would cover me like a soft blanket.

His eyes remained closed as I read, and his hand unconsciously fell to his lap.

I watched her go down the steps, with the hurried walk of a young girl. As she moved away, she quickly looked back toward my window. With the knee-jerk reflex of a man caught spying, I felt a blush of shame, something I wasn't used to feeling. In that moment, I saw her face for the first time. Now in those days, an almost 30-year-old unmarried woman still at home was what we called an old maid or a spinster—and they usually looked it. Not her. And those eyes! Later I saw the beauty and depth in those eyes, which were always alluring, but changed with her moods:

clear blue and bright with light when she was laughing or play-
ful; a muted, soft green when she was sad or pensive; smoky gray
and catlike, after we were intimate. She would look into my eyes
then and tell me she loved me. And I would believe her. And I
would grow to love her as much as a man like me ever could.

I looked at him. His eyes were closed, but not as tight. I stayed
quiet, to let him enjoy the visit with the girl from his day. His face
was placid, with no trace of pain. I saw no trace of joy, either.
Instead his skin looked frozen, as if injected with formaldehyde.
Minutes passed and his stillness unnerved me; a sudden heave of
his chest came as a relief. He hadn't died before my eyes.

"Life is not only for the living, but for the dead who were loved
by them," he said. "Keep reading, if you want. But not out loud. Let
me rest."

That first glimpse of her aroused my curiosity, but the
Lindbergh case was go, go, go. I would get back to the Lawson
house well after midnight, sometimes not much before dawn. By
eight or nine the next morning, I was at it again.

After a few days of watching, I tried to bump into her on the
street. "No meals" meant the rest of the house was off-limits to me.
I was the stranger upstairs, the man who came in the front door
and went straight to his room; the man whose footsteps were
heard but whose face was never seen. So, I got up early and
walked to town, had a cup of coffee and two pieces of toast in the
coffee shop, and at 7:20 began heading back to the house. As I
turned the corner onto Second Street, I saw her come down the
steps. My heart giddyapped as she came toward me, walking fast,
head down, intent on getting wherever she was going. We were on
a collision course and I had my opening line all rehearsed:

"You don't know me, but I live with you!"

She had an athletic, determined gait; shoulders and hips in perfect alignment. There was rhythm and power in her stride. With all that churning strength coming straight at me, I began to doubt my ability to slow her down with my flimsy opening line.

When she was within fifty feet of me, she suddenly veered off and crossed the street, without even a glance in my direction. What could I do? Follow her? I would have looked over-anxious.

Instead, I tried again the next day, delaying my arrival time on Second Street until she would have crossed. This time, I missed her entirely.

On the third day, I was about to leave the coffee house, when she came in. She ordered a container of coffee at the register, and I stood next to her there, waiting to pay my bill. When the cash register lady handed her the coffee and said, "There you go, Miz Lawson," I had my opening.

"Lawson? My landlord's name is Lawson—over on Second Street." She turned to look at me.

"You must be the newspaperman upstairs."

"Frederick G. Haines, New York Daily Mirror," I said and stuck my hand out. Her handshake was firm as her father's. I dropped her hand and couldn't think of a single thing to say.

After a moment of awkward silence, she rescued me.

"So, Mr. Haines, what does the 'G' stand for?"

Now in the past whenever I would get asked that question, my reflex would be to lie. George, I would say. Don't ask me why I lied ... maybe because I didn't want to admit the G stood for nothing, that Frederick G. Haines was a made-up moniker—the name of a part-fictional character, the guy in the newspaper.

But now with Miss Lawson's eyes penetrating me to root out my ruse, I felt the truth spill out before I had a chance to stop it.

"The G?" I said. "It stands for nothing. I made it up a long time ago to make me sound more official. The truth is I don't have a middle name."

"That's odd," she said.

"That I don't have a middle name?" I asked.

"That you would make one up."

"Well, I guess it is, now that you mention it," I said. I felt myself blushing, of all things. "I guess that's why I never told anybody before. You're the first person to know my secret."

I waited for her to respond, or at least ask why I chose to tell her—a question for which I had no prepared answer.

Instead, she just said, "Well, it was nice meeting you, Mr. Haines," and turned to leave.

I threw my money on the counter—a whole buck for a nickel cup of coffee and a ten-cent order of toast—and hurried out after her.

"You know, you can call me Fred or Freddy. And if you give me half a chance, you might find out the G stands for Good Guy," I said.

"That would be two Gs, then," she said.

I laughed.

"You must be a schoolteacher," I said.

"Why, because I can count to two?"

"No, because you like to correct people."

"I do that in my work," she said.

"Correct people?"

"And count to two ... I'm a bookkeeper." And then she gave me her fabulous smile.

I walked her three blocks to her job at an in-town insurance broker. We made small talk, mostly about the Lindbergh case. At the door, I asked her name.

"Sara."

Then I asked if I could see her again.

"Sure. You can see me around," she said, then lingered for a moment before going into work, like a schoolgirl being dropped off from a first date, giving a boy a chance to think about a goodnight kiss, then snatching the moment away. And, boy, I wanted to, because that three-minute walk from the coffee shop to her office was the best first date I ever had.

For the next few days, I managed to bump into her at the coffee shop, then walk her to work. Our pace slowed a little each day. She asked me about life in New York, the newspaper business, and the Lindbergh investigation. These were not questions of a small town girl, bored with her little Hicksville and the Simpletons in it. No, they were questions of someone who was as sharp and worldly as a place like Hopewell allowed her to be.

One morning, I asked her why she stayed.

"Certainly, there must be opportunities for bookkeepers in New York or Philadelphia, or even Trenton, for God sakes."

"When I was little, I used to dream someone would come and take me away into the world. It never happened. And now, with this Lindbergh situation, the world has come to me."

"So are you still waiting for someone to take you away?"

"This is my home," she said. "I'm comfortable here."

I asked her if I could take her on an official date.

"No, Freddy. I think you're a nice enough guy, but already I can feel people in town watching us. Pretty soon, they'll be talking. My parents ... my father, really, wouldn't approve. He says you can't trust a New Yorker and you especially can't trust a newspaperman. He says if you can't believe what they say in the paper, how can you believe what they say to your face?"

Later that night, I came home earlier than usual from the Lindbergh estate. As I pulled up, I noticed a faint light from a downstairs room on the side of the house. It struck me as odd because usually when I got there, the house was all dark except for a porch light they left on for me. I pulled the car 'round back and started walking up front.

From the dimly lit room, I caught a glimpse of shadowy movement, so I stopped and looked. It was Sara, behind a screen of lace curtains in a room lit only by a candle. This had been the dining room, now converted to her bedroom to make room for the boarder. The windows were almost floor to ceiling, designed for light, not privacy.

I stopped and watched her. She was wearing a pale yellow robe, and she was brushing her hair steadily, studying herself in the mirror of the dining room buffet. The light, the lace curtain, everything around her looked golden. A heavenly glow, surrounding an angel. An angel being watched by a devil!

I was ashamed of myself, but the sheer excitement of watching her overpowered my shame. She put down the brush and began to fiddle with the robe sash. I knew what was coming, and I wanted to turn away, but couldn't. My head was light, and I felt a slight buzzing in my ears.

The robe came undone and hung open, still covering her breasts but exposing the patch of her private area. There was a basin on the buffet, and she reached in, took out a washcloth, squeezed it, and washed herself. She was thorough and not as gentle as you'd expect. I couldn't take my eyes off her. My face and ears were hot from the simultaneous sensations of arousal and shame. She rinsed the rag and did it again, just as thorough, but a little longer. Oh, what a show! I wanted it to last forever, and I wanted it to end. The only feeling stronger than my arousal was my fear of getting caught. I looked both ways, slunk back into the shadows. Then, in one quick motion, she took the robe off. I moved back closer to the window to take her all in.

Her neck was elegant, her naked shoulders broad but grace-
fully slight, her back was long and trim, her hipline perfectly
curved, like the body of a guitar crafted by Padre Eterno himself.
She gave herself a once-over in the mirror as I stared hard at her,
trying to make an indelible imprint of her naked body in my
memory, a mental pin-up picture I could take out and look at over
and over again, like some love-starved schoolboy with a stash of
naughty pictures under his mattress.

When she was done washing, she grabbed her nightgown off
the buffet, pulled it over her head, and dropped it over her body
like a curtain coming down on the show. As she moved to blow
out the candle, I slunk down the driveway, where I paused to
catch my breath.

To see and not be seen is part of the reporter's makeup.
Voyeurism is a dirty word, but it is what it is. I thought of times in
my own life, beginning with Aunt Mag in her underwear to my
intrusive question to Sister Lucia to my life as a reporter at the
Shore Record. I thought of all the stories, from police funerals to
criminal sentencings, where I would watch the grieving or the
guilty, observing details for the next day's story. The fly on the wall,
the potted plant, call it what you will. Often, I thought, is this
curiosity at work, or something less desirable? To see and not be
seen is also part of a sniper's makeup.

I continued reading.

For the next few days, I cut short my eavesdropping routine at
Lindbergh's so I could get home earlier to spy on Sara. Each
night was as exhilarating as the first. I wanted to get closer; I
wanted to love her naked body. Then I would wake up early and
rush off to intercept her at the coffee shop, walk her to work, and

ask if she would meet me for dinner or an evening walk. She was as consistent in turning me down as I was persistent in asking. This went on for a week, and I continued to fall for her. I longed for her company and ached for her body. I was ashamed of my spying, but I couldn't bring myself to stop.

One night I returned home to find her room already dark. I went to my room, undressed and lay down on the bed. A few minutes later, I heard soft footsteps on the stairs, then the rustle of paper under my door. It was a simple note: "Meet me in the park. —S."

The park was a block down Second Street, and I found her sitting on a bench under a young oak, bundled up in her navy coat. The lightness of her hair in the moonlight and the glow of a cigarette gave her away. It was late March, still cold as bejesus, and I saw her shiver as I approached.

"I come out here to smoke some nights, especially in spring and summer," she said. "I thought you might like to join me."

"I'm glad you asked," I said. "But I didn't know you smoked."

"I don't, really. Not at home and not in public. Just here, sometimes, at night. When I want to be alone."

"Do you want to be alone tonight?"

"I asked you to come, didn't I?"

I sat next to her but didn't light a cigarette—I didn't want to delay the inevitable another second. She must have felt the same way because she bent down to crush hers out after one more puff. She hadn't straightened fully when I kissed her. Right away, a deep kiss. My tongue danced with hers, my lips smashed against her lips. I held her head with one hand and slipped the other hand under her coat, feeling the curve of her hip and narrowness of her waist, and then bringing it to rest on the underbelly of her breasts. We lost our breath at the same time and broke for air. I pulled her head close to mine and inhaled deeply in her hair, trying to breathe her all in—something I had never done before and haven't done with another woman since. We kissed like that, then talked, and then kissed some more, oblivious to the cold, protected by the darkness.

Later that night, she snuck up to my room in her bare feet, wearing only the nightgown I had seen her put on night after night. She came to my bed, gathered up the nightgown around her hips and slowly lowered herself on me.

I put the manuscript down, and looked at the old man sleeping in his wheelchair. For the first time, I saw the mask of his rollicking stories. *Rollicking,* his word. A word that meant the good times; a word that buried the hidden context of pain. Then I closed my eyes, to digest it all for a few minutes, and Fred Haines and I took a nap together.

***

"Tell me, kid, have you ever been in love?" Haines was awake. Groggy, but ready to resume.

"Once or twice, maybe three times," I said. "Truth is, I'm not sure what it is. The second truth is, newspapermen make lousy husbands, and the women I've known knew that."

As the years went by, I often found myself consumed by the daily story. Not just me, but most of my colleagues. It took a while but I figured it out: We yielded our personal lives to the news because it was emotionally easier and safer that way. The hard part of life is not work; it's finding and maintaining love. I walked away from it, or shut it out those few, precious times I saw it coming. The daily, draining challenge of chasing news was a great excuse for standing on the sidelines of the game that mattered most. I said all this to Haines.

"That's for damn sure!" he said, with a surprising laugh. "A great newspaperman only has room in his heart for the story. He lives for the deadline, addicted to the adrenaline of the chase. I met lots of girls in my time, but only one who made me want to give it up.

"You know, fellas your age always think your generation was the first to discover sex. But there was plenty of sex in my day, my friend. Plenty. And I had more than my share. I met plenty of girls as a tabloid hustler: speakeasy girls, dance hall girls, and a couple of girls who hoofed their way up to Broadway. There was the neglected wife of a beat cop I knew, a good source he was, and the lonely boozer girlfriend of my regular bartender. There were some regular working girls—a teller at the bank around the corner from the *Mirror* and a salesgirl from Macy's, both impressed that I knew Winchell, and a couple of female reporters at the *Daily News* and the *Mirror*. Then there was Bernarr Macfadden's 'personal assistant' at the *Daily Graphic*, a strong-lady who lifted barbells and once confided to me that Macfadden's most impressive muscle was his bicep. There was a Czech violinist with the Manhattan Philharmonic who shared a one-bedroom apartment with a Hungarian cellist, one more beautiful than the other, and, well, never let anyone tell you Eastern European women are dull and unadventurous!

"I could go on, but you get my point. Some of these were affairs of the heart, and some were … not. I'd been in love a few times and in lust plenty.

"And, so here's the difference between love and lust: I never felt anything like Sara Lawson slowly lowering herself on me. Everything about her was a perfect fit. She slid down on me and when she got to the end we both shuddered. She fell into my arms, tickling my face with her hair, and our bodies came together like contiguous pieces of a flesh and bone puzzle. Everything fit! There was no protruding rib bone or hip bone to distract us. Her shoulders and back were made for my arms. Our ribcages and bellies were contoured to match. Our legs intertwined like braided rope."

He stopped, and I filled the void of silence—again, his expression—by saying something inane like, "It sounds perfect."

"Perfect, in that moment. But beyond that, too," he said. "I always heard there was 'someone for everyone.' Of course, I didn't believe it. People got married out of convenience, or in a desperate attempt to combat loneliness and fill the emptiness of otherwise miserable lives. They procreated because it was expected of them and hoped their children would lead the fulfilling lives that had passed them by.

"Not me. I wasn't falling for it. I didn't believe in life-sentence commitment and certainly didn't want to become some woman's house husband. Nope. I was going to carouse as long as I could and cajole as many women into bed as possible. I had the right job for it, too. A tabloid guy was on the street, meeting all sorts, moving day to day, story to story, like an actor in a traveling show. Girls were just part of the menagerie. With every other girl I've known, the minute the thrill was over I couldn't wait to get moving. With Sara, I wanted her to stay close to me, I wanted to touch as much of her body as I could with my body. In those dreamy moments, I would find ways to cover her as much as I could without suffocating her. She said it made her feel safe, and no words ever made me feel so protective."

"So deep down inside, you have a chivalrous soul," I offered.

Haines laughed. "I never thought of it that way, but maybe. All I know is being that close also made me feel secure, and comforted, too. I told her more than once that if I could hold her like that for eternity, I would have taken death right then and there.

"When Sara finally said, '*I love you, Freddy*' to me in her soft moan, it was a voice that reached deep in my soul, like one of God's angels beckoning me to join her in the afterlife. My whole life I wanted 'I love you' to sound like that. It never had before Sara, and it never did again.

"In all those long years after Sara was gone from my life, when everything was still and I was alone, night after night, year after year, I could still hear *her* voice. Even now, all these decades later, with my mortality bearing down on me, when my lungs rattle and I'm not sure if morning is coming around, I hear her voice—'*I love you, Freddy,*'—and I believe she is waiting for me. Then I wake up and I miss her, and all she took with her, all over again. And when I close my eyes at night I can feel her again. Do you have any idea what that is like?"

"No, I don't," I said. "Not really."

"I'm glad for you."

9

The old man blinked his magnified eyes rapidly. The "something" in his eyes was not tears, but he took a crumpled napkin from his robe pocket and wiped anyway. Then he looked at the napkin and saw it was dry. He appeared to be crying, but no tears came. He was dried up. I stayed quiet, out of respect for his grief, and because I had nothing to say. I knew loss, through death. An accepted fact of life. Haines's loss seemed more painful. His ghost lived for decades, out of his reach, but still there. My pain was thrust on me; his came from the inside out. Mine diminished with time; his was buried deep in his soul and grew over time. I felt sorry for the guy. So old, and still nursing a broken heart, vulnerable to the end.

Finally, for lack of anything better I said, "I'm sorry."

"You probably think I'm a sentimental old fool."

"Old, yes," I said, attempting levity.

He laughed a little. "Old I am. *And* a fool, sometimes, but rarely sentimental. Only when it comes to Sara Lawson."

The relationship, for the three months or so that it lasted, was secret; and so it remained for 67 years.

"She didn't want to be seen running around with a newspaperman, and I didn't want the newspaper guys thinking of her as a traveling salesman joke—as just some broad Freddy laid while her old man was snoring away downstairs, loaded shotgun by his side. She was much too good for that.

"Even after it was over, I didn't tell a living soul. I kept protecting her. That, and I didn't want to rip the scab off my own wound— guess I didn't have the courage. So I locked her away like some precious jewel stashed in a safe deposit box. She's been locked away so long now that I wonder if she really existed the way I remember, or if I've just reduced her to a paper-thin character—a princess—the same way my stories reduced Lindbergh and Hauptmann to hero and villain."

"And no other woman ever came along to help you put it in perspective?" I asked.

"About ten years later, I got quite close to another woman, but there was nothing like the passion I had for Sara. She could tell, of course, and had to let me go. At the end she asked, 'Who is the woman who hurt you? The woman you put so high on a pedestal that no one else can compete? Tell me about her, and I'll explain why she wasn't real.'

"I lied to her and said there was no one. She knew better. You can't fool women that way. She told me, 'You can't hide behind her forever, Freddy. Let her go. If not, you'll end up sad and alone.' She was right. But I never did. I never could. For awhile, I didn't have to. The treadmill of tabloid life kept me busy, running day-to-day, story-to-story. In the '40s, a few years after I quit the newspaper, there were enough war brides, then war widows, to keep a man like me on the move.

"But as I got older, and the women didn't come by as often, I spent my evenings longing for what I'd lost, and what I'd never had. I imagined us together. I could hear her voice and even feel her touch as I lay alone at night sometimes. She was alive to me, but I never reached out for her, and I never spoke of her."

"So why now? Why tell me?" I asked.

Again, he looked out the window and took a deep breath, as if he needed one gulp of air to dilute the apparition of her he kept locked in his chest. He exhaled loudly, as if he were trying to evict her, then turned back to me and said calmly, "Well, actually, you're not the first. I told Hauptmann."

"Hauptmann? Why Hauptmann, of all people?" I asked, and I knew it sounded like I didn't believe him.

"Keep reading and you'll get to it eventually," Haines said. "It's all part of 'Bruno's Confession.'"

After that first night, she would appear in my room other times without warning, love me, then leave again as quietly as she came.

Each morning, I would meet her in the coffee shop and walk her to work. One day as I said goodbye at her office, she looked both ways then kissed me quick on the cheek—that was the closest we ever came to being what Winchell called a "public item."

In the park one night, she told me about her family farm out in Mount Airy, a little rural village seven miles west of Hopewell.

"My dad was raised there," she said, "and his older sister, my Aunt Margie, lived there her whole life until she died a few months ago. I go there on weekends to get things in order. You could meet me. We would be safe, because I take the family car, leaving my folks pretty much stranded in town."

The farm was about twenty-five acres of fallow land. There hadn't been any farming since Sara's grandfather passed away, so the fields were mostly overrun with tall grass and weeds, and there were no animals at all except local critters like deer, raccoons, skunks, and foxes. The house was plain, a little run-down like the grounds, and set off the road a bit, surrounded by a few cedars and overgrown shrubbery. I'd park my car around back, behind an old barn.

It was a raw spring, and the first thing we would do is light a fire. Sara taught me how to build it. Paper, usually yesterday's

Daily Mirror, *topped by kindling of little dry twigs, then topped by bigger twigs and sticks. After that got going good, I'd put on one quartered log, then another. Once I learned how, I loved to build fires into roaring infernos that warmed the whole house. There was no shortage of firewood in the barn—old Aunt Margie chopped wood till the day she died. And there was no shortage of paper, since I picked up the* Mirror *every day to check my stories.*

At Mount Airy, we were free to be domestic, to do things other couples took for granted. Like prepare a simple dinner. Take a little walk in the woods. Sit on the couch and listen to the Philco or Victrola. Her aunt had Enrico Caruso records, and one night I put Pagliacci on the turntable, climbed on the coffee table with a funnel on my head, puffed out my gut, and did an exaggerated impression of the crying clown. Oh, how that made her laugh!

That's why she fell for me, I think. I was an entertaining New York wise guy. A guy with a million stories, who walked aside famous people, who talked a good game, fast and funny. The small-town people she knew were dull. They talked about weather, crop prices, and strangers in town. They were colorless. Me, I was effusive in complimenting her looks, unabashed in expressing my love. She probably had never heard anyone talk like me, and she always gushed that my words made her feel beautiful. And I was a guy not afraid to be a crying clown.

We carried on like newlyweds every weekend we spent in that house. Sometimes after dinner, we would sit by the fire wrapped in Aunt Margie's stuffed comforters, and I would imagine myself settling down in a podunk town like Mount Airy or Hopewell, becoming a countrified gent, talking about things like frost and feed costs. I knew I'd be as foreign there as she would be in New York, but—what the hell?—I'd try it for her.

It was under those comforters in the glow of those fires that I told her about New York, and the news business, and the big stories I'd been on.

She found some things objectionable, like us getting the shot of Ruth Snyder in the chair. I told her about the terrible things I saw on the job, the crimes and tragedies, and she asked me, "How do you keep your humanity in the face of such things? When you see nothing but the bad things life has to offer, it has to affect your outlook."

I read that last line again, then read it out loud to Haines.

"We are what we become," I said. "We become what we are."

"I don't follow," he said.

"Me and you, we're newspapermen," I said. "We spread the crimes and tragedies but ignore the better side of humanity. What do we call news? The dark anomalies of life. A house burns down. A child is hit by a car. A husband murders his wife. On the way to those stories, we pass thousands of standing houses, with happy children and couples. But what do we call the 'good story' in the newsroom? We don't accurately report on society, because we focus on the negative. Eventually, society sees only the negative in the paper or on TV. But they see all the other positive things around them. So they realize the paper or TV news isn't accurate, so it can't be trusted, so it becomes irrelevant. Sara was right, more right than she ever knew."

Haines thought it over.

"Now that you mention it, maybe her question wasn't a question; maybe it was an observation. Maybe she saw less humanity in me than she needed in a man. It was an observation, a prediction, too, and I proved her right with the Lindbergh baby photo. It's all in there. Keep reading."

When she fell asleep in my arms, it moved me to tears. Once, my tears spilled onto her face and woke her. She thought it was sweet. When I held her and drifted into sleep, I dreamt our souls merged; mine was a deep color, a purple or red, and hers was much lighter. They would come together and make a beautiful shade of lavender or rose.

One night, she woke me and said, "I know as soon as this Lindbergh business is over, you'll leave here and forget all about me. And I want you to know, that's all right."

When she said this, she didn't sound sad, she sounded practical.

"Come back to New York with me," I said. "You'll love it there."

"But I'm comfortable here," she would say. "I'm comfortable with my life."

"Then I'll stay here, with you."

"Freddy, there's not enough here to keep you happy. When you tell your stories ..."

I held my finger to her lips. "You're here."

"No. I'm not enough."

She fell asleep then, and I later realized that if she dreamt of our souls, hers was white and mine was black, and she couldn't live with those shades of gray. She couldn't live with a man who published pictures of a dead baby.

These pictures caused quite a controversy all across the country. The sales proved it, some 2 million, and other papers from New York to Chicago to Los Angeles and London and Paris ran editorials decrying our taste. But no one was as offended as the good folks of Hopewell, who were appalled that we could be so crass, so indifferent to the Lindberghs' feelings. They were protective of the Lindberghs; they were neighbors, after all, even though few in town had ever laid eyes on them.

The morning the paper came out, I met Sara as usual. She hadn't seen it yet, and I damn sure wasn't going to bring it up.

That night, when I came back to my room after being smacked around by Henning, there was a note under the door: Meet me in the park. *I knew what was coming.*

"Freddy! How could you? An innocent baby. A baby! His poor mother!" she said.

And she began to cry. Hard.

I felt like a monster. I began to make my "it's news" defense, but decided the best thing to do was just sit there quiet. I put my arm around her shoulder and she leaned into me, crying tears for the dead and unborn.

"Sara, I know it was wrong, but I had no choice," I said, hating the cowardice in my own voice.

"If you knew it was wrong, then you had a choice," she shot back. "A baby! An innocent baby!"

I had never seen her so upset, and I was struck by the intensity of her reaction. She pulled her arms tight around her waist, as if she had a stomachache, and rocked.

"How could you!" she said again.

Her tears bruised me more than Henning's punches and her sobs took my breath away like his shot to my solar plexus.

"Sara, I love you." I couldn't think of anything else to say.

She looked at me with an expression that was part fear, part fight, as if I were a stranger who had startled her in the dark park.

"That doesn't make it all right, Freddy."

I shut up for good then. A few minutes later I walked her home, my heart sinking with every step, afraid she was through with me.

Later that night, I was surprised when she came to me. But instead of showing me her usual tenderness, she rode me rough, as if she was trying to rip herself up inside. The bed creaked and groaned beneath us, and she was moaning, loud, but in pain not pleasure.

The next night, the same thing happened.

"Please stop this," I whispered, desperate. I imagined her father bursting in on us, gun in hand, and my own obituary was running through my head: "Frederick G. Haines, the *New York Daily Mirror* tabloid reporter who gave the public the pictures of the rotted body of the Lindbergh baby was shot and killed last night in Hopewell, New Jersey, by the angry father of an innocent girl he seduced … and the world is better for it."

She broke down in tears and left.

The next two days, I missed her at the coffee shop. She was avoiding me, and it was driving me crazy. The second night she came to my room.

"I have something important to tell you," she said as her voice quivered.

"Tell me now," I said.

"No, Saturday at the farm."

"Please."

"No. At the farm."

On Saturday in Mount Airy, I found her at the kitchen table with a cup of tea, looking worn and worried, but strangely full in the face—swollen from crying, I thought—and more beautiful than ever. She had scrambled up a batch of eggs and fried some bacon but told me she couldn't wait and had eaten without me.

I said something like, "I'm only hungry for you," pulled her to her feet and kissed her hard. I told her I loved her.

She said, "I love you, too, Freddy. But, right now, I must be sure I know who you are."

I tried to explain there were two of me, the newspaper hustler and … well, I couldn't really say who the "other me" was, except he wasn't like the newspaper hustler.

Worse, the more I tried to explain the "other me," the more she questioned how the kind, sensitive me, a man worthy of her affections, could co-exist in the same body with the newspaper hustler.

The more I tried to explain, the more questions she threw at me. She was prosecuting me, her Freddy, for the crimes of Frederick G. Haines of the New York Daily Mirror.

I confessed that, yes, there were times I capitalized, even reveled in the misfortune of others because it made a good story. I admitted my paper's stock-in-trade was blood and guts and salacious details. I confessed to having ignored and even bent the truth to make a story more unsavory. Worst of all, I admitted I had fun doing it—up till now. I said I would quit it all for her.

I saw her face soften, so I kept confessing. I cried that I was repulsed by my actions over the baby photographs. I would change, I told her. I was tired of sticking my nose in other people's business, of the sneaking around, of the standing in the shadows, whether it was eavesdropping on Schwarzkopf, spying on the Lindberghs, or spying on her.

And I will never forget the expression that overtook her face. It was as if I had just punched her in the gut for no reason.

"What do you mean, spying on me?"

I said nothing. What do say when you see your life going down the drain?

"Freddy, what do you mean, spying on me?" she repeated.

I told her. I told her the truth. I confessed how I stood in the shadows night after night, watching her bedtime routine. I tried to apologize, but she cut me off.

"What is this, then? What is all this?" she shrieked. "Some sick Peeping Tom fantasy? You said you loved me, and now you tell me this?!"

I tried to hug her, but she stiffened and turned away. I grabbed her shoulder, but she shrugged free.

"Sara, I—"

"Don't!" she said, backing away. "Don't say anything. I have to think about things, Freddy. I have a lot to think about now, Freddy."

She covered her face with her hands and asked me to leave, and I knew she was gone.

A few days later, I watched as she packed a few bags into the car and drove off with her father. It was mid-May, but cold and drizzling. I climbed under the comforter and slept the day away, thinking how empty my arms felt. The next morning, the car was back but there was no Sara going off to work, no Sara at the coffee shop.

That night, I drove to Mount Airy and saw lights on behind the shades. But I didn't stop, not wanting to upset or frighten her.

Saturday morning at Mount Airy, she came to the back door as soon as I pulled the car around. She had been crying and there was a sick feeling in the pit of my stomach. I knew whatever was about to happen wasn't going to be good.

I was right. She dumped me.

She talked about us "not being right for each other" and "how she had to think of the future."

She told me it would be easier for us both if I left her alone.

"A gentleman would do that," she said.

"I'll be a gentleman, then."

I told her I would move out of her father's house so she could come back.

She told me it wouldn't be necessary, because she planned to stay at the farm.

I would move anyway, I said, there were too many memories in my room.

She agreed, and said she would always remember me fondly.

And I told her I would love her forever.

And that was that.

I stopped reading.

"You gave up," I said. "You didn't fight for her. What happened to the old Haines swagger? What happened to 'showtime'? That was completely out of character for you."

"There!" Haines came up in his chair, with sudden enthusiasm. "You just answered your own question. It *was* out of character. My 'character' would have barged back in and schmoozed and cajoled and manipulated. But I didn't know how to do any of that from the heart, with sincerity. That's what she wanted to see, and I couldn't deliver. I tried, but failed. I couldn't pull it off. It wasn't in my actor's repertoire. What was it you said before? 'We are what we become?' Well, hell, that was me. But in the end, by not fighting for her, maybe I became something better. You'll see if you keep reading."

Within 24 hours, I moved into another house on the other side of town. After the baby was found, the investigation heated up, and I was plenty busy. Then His Highness Winchell got to town. Winchell tried to treat me like his house boy, but I was having none of it. My pipeline, Henning, was now dry, but I kept running hard to break stories, mostly to not think about Sara.

A few weeks went by, and the cold spring was finally giving way to summer. One day, I saw her come out of Frelinger's Drugstore, where I bought my cigarettes. I picked up my pace to catch her, but ducked into a doorway when she was joined by a young man—a kid, really, no more than 21 or 22. I recognized him from the store. They walked away together, but stopped to greet a middle-aged woman. I saw the young man gently pat Sara's shoulder as the three exchanged pleasantries, and she took his arm as they walked away.

I went into the drugstore to buy my Pall Malls. The druggist, Mr. Frelinger, was behind the counter.

"*That young man you have working here, the one I just saw on the street. He's a nice fella. Always very polite and helpful.*"

"*That's my son, Jimmy,*" the druggist said. "*Just got himself a nice girlfriend, too.*"

I stopped going to Frelinger's.

A few weeks later, I saw old man Lawson in town. I tried to avoid him, but he spotted me.

"*Hey, Mr. Haines! How's news?*" he said, slapping me on the back like a favorite son-in-law.

"*News is news,*" I said. "*It keeps happening.*"

"*Well, I got some news of my own. My Sara is getting married.*"

I smiled with the false bravado of a prizefighter who's just been punched in the teeth and is trying to convince his opponent it didn't hurt.

"*Yessir. She's marrying Jimmy Frelinger. His father owns the drugstore, and the boy is already trained in the art of the apothecary. In fact, he just mixed me up a tonic to settle my jitters. The wedding is Saturday!*"

"*That's kind of sudden, isn't it?*" *I blurted.*

He looked at me a bit curiously but kept talking.

"*I guess love just can't wait,*" he said. "*You know, my girl's no spring chicken, so the sooner the better. And it's quite a story! She used to babysit this boy, and he used to follow her around like a lost puppy. Now they're getting married. That's some love story! Maybe you want to write about something nice like that and take a break from all that claptrap about the Lindberghs.*"

"*Well, that's wonderful news,*" I managed. "*Congratulations.*"

I started on my way, but he caught my elbow.

"*You oughta stop by. Sara mentioned she bumped into you a few times in town and thought you was quite a character,*" he said. "*The wedding's nothing fancy. We're having a picnic reception at our family farm in Mount Airy. It ain't hard to find.*"

I told him thanks, but I was leaving town. The Lindberghs had left Hopewell and moved back to Mrs. Lindbergh's father's mansion in Englewood. She was expecting their second child and felt safer there. The state police had also vacated the Lindbergh house and gone back to Trenton, and everybody from J. Edgar Hoover down was calling for the FBI and NYPD to take over the case. I was headed back to New York.

I shook old man Lawson's hand and asked him to congratulate his daughter for me. I thanked him for his hospitality, and we shook hands one final time.

I drove out to Mount Airy that night. There was a car in the driveway, presumably Jimmy's, and there were lights on in the house. I parked down the road, waiting to see if he would leave. I waited, smoking cigarette after cigarette, till after midnight, when the house lights went out.

The next night I did the same thing. I decided to try my luck during the day. Jimmy's car wasn't there, so I parked my car in plain sight and knocked on the front door. She came out wearing a flower print frock. I remember how creamy and full her skin looked and how much I wanted to kiss it. Her hair, usually golden, looked a shade darker.

"I came out to say good-bye and wish you luck," I said. "I saw your father, and he told me you were getting married."

She lowered her head and bit her lip. "I am, Freddy. Thank you. I wish you luck, too."

"I don't need luck, Sara. I need you." I weakened and grabbed at her like she was a life preserver.

"Please don't," she said and backed away. "Please—I can't …"

We heard a car on the road, and both turned to see Jimmy Frelinger coming 'round the bend. I backed off to the bottom step, a respectable distance.

He pulled in the driveway and got out. He didn't seem alarmed to see a strange man on the porch with his wife-to-be, because, like the song said, he only had eyes for her. That kid was just beaming at my Sara, my love.

He gave her a big hello and a big hug. She introduced us and explained I was the newspaperman who had lived upstairs at her father's.

I didn't miss a beat. I said I was headed back to New York and just stopped by to wish them good luck, having heard the wonderful news from her father. Even in lies, Sara and I were in rhythm. Jimmy turned and shook my outstretched hand with the firm handshake of an Eagle Scout.

And then I saw it.

He had one arm around her, and the other dropped unconsciously to her belly, where he gently rubbed a growing pouch.

"Thank you, Mr. Haines," he said, all earnest. "Sara and I are very happy."

My eyes moved to Sara's, which turned smoky. I thought I saw in her eyes the same look she gave me in our most intimate moments.

Or was it a shroud over some sadness she had to hide? What were those eyes asking me? "Remember our passion now and take me away" *or* "Please, go now and forget me forever."

I didn't know then, and I don't know now.

All I know is I had a handful of uncomfortable ticks on the clock ... just a few beats of the human heart ... to make a decision about the rest of our lives.

What did she want from me?

To claim what was mine and, damn the scandal, sweep her off her feet and into our future?

Or to bow out, broken heart and all, retreat back to New York, and let her forget we ever happened?

Did she want me to be courageous or a coward?
And which way meant which?
I picked the easy way.
Out.
I wished them well and walked back to my car, walked back into a life I was comfortable with. The newspaper life. Lurking in the shadows, telling stories that weren't mine.

I felt I was shrinking with every step. I was afraid that by the time I got to the car, I would be reduced to schoolboy size, unable to see over the wheel. I heard the front door of the house shut behind me, a heavy slam, a prison-door slam confining me to life without her. I got in the car and drove away a safe distance from the house and pulled over. I sat there, not like Frederick G. Haines, big city newspaperman, but like the Freddy I am, and cried.

As I read, Fred Haines stared out the window, looking at nothing but shadowy ghosts of an ancient past, a history neither dead nor alive to anyone but him.

When I finished and looked up from the pages, he waved his hand at me before I could speak. A dismissal for the day. The old guy was drained. His sadness brought out the frailty of his age, and I wanted to protect him.

"We can stop," I said. "We can talk about something else."

"There is nothing else." He turned on me. "Haven't you been listening?"

He quickly apologized.

"Sorry, kid. I just need a break from this," he said. "Come back tomorrow. Take me for a ride. Take me to the boardwalk. There are a few places I'd like to see again, one last time, and I'll tell you the rest of the story."

10

When I arrived the next day, Haines was in the solarium entertaining the women, who laughed and flirted with him like middle school girls. The old guy still had it. I spied for while, happy for him and wondering if some of his charisma could ever rub off on me.

When he saw me, he rolled up in a compact, travel-size wheelchair. Instead of his royal blue robe, he was bundled up in a trench coat and on his head was a gray felt fedora with a black band.

"All that's missing is the press card," I said, motioning just above the hat brim.

"Never carried one. Made you stick out like a sore thumb. I preferred to blend in. See and not be seen, isn't that what you said?"

On his lap was a heavy Oceanview-issue blanket, coarse wool, like the Army kind. On top of that was a bagged lunch.

"You got to sign for me," he said. "Like a piece of baggage."

I signed him out and pushed him to my car. When we got to the passenger door, he locked the chair and extended a hand.

"Help me up."

He pulled himself up on my grip, and his strength surprised me. Using the open door, he guided himself into the seat.

"Easy as pie," he said.

I folded the chair and stashed it in the trunk.

"Drive to the beach," he said when I got in. A few blocks later, we could see the ocean as it rose to meet the sky on the horizon.

It was early December, still mild, but the Jersey Shore towns were left to their scant year-round residents. Through Bradley Beach and Avon-by-the-Sea, Ocean Avenue was pleasantly deserted. The band shell was silent, its benches empty. The only music now was the wind whistling as it dusted the sand off the streets. The arcades and bars in Belmar were boarded up for winter; the kids who trashed the town were home in Staten Island and North Jersey or back in college. Only the hardiest joggers and dog walkers were out on the boardwalk. The whole place seemed sanitized.

"Go down to Spring Lake," he said. "All the way to the South End; that's where the ship burned. And put the windows down. Let me breathe in some of this good salt air."

In late fall, the veil of humidity along the Jersey coast is lifted as the wind shifts from southeast to northwest. The mist blows out, rather than in. As we drove toward Spring Lake, windows open, the crisp, salty breeze invigorated Haines and brought a youthful blush to his face.

"Look at Big Blue," he said pointing to the ocean. "Magnificent!" I agreed.

"Funny, I only learned to appreciate it covering the *Morro Castle* disaster," he said. "Drive down the beach. I'll show you."

He was quiet for a moment, then said, "That experience changed me. It taught me two valuable lessons. The first, which I finally got through my thick head, is that newspapering is a cynical and facetious business, except when skepticism gets in the way of a tidy, pat story. I was guilty of that plenty, but the worst was down here, when I made a valiant hero of a heinous villain.

"The second is there is nothing heroic or glorious about sitting on the sidelines. Oh, all of us self-important newsmen! We act like reporting is as noble as participating. We pretend that criticizing is as important as creating. Winchell was a new breed—a self-serving news messenger who thought he was as important as the news maker. And there's been no shortage of his kind since. Let me tell you, our business is populated by frauds, and nothing exposes them as does a true calamity, like the *Morro Castle*. And like the Lindbergh kidnapping, too, which was solved not by the millions of words written by a pack of press dogs, but by the hard work of one dedicated detective.

"Tell me about the detective," I said, but I needn't have asked. Haines was energized, eager to talk, his sadness over Sara Lawson once again locked down deep inside.

"You asked me the other day if I *knew* Hauptmann was guilty. I said, yes, because he told me so. But even without Bruno's confession, I would have known, because I was there, step-for-step with the cop who solved the case. And no matter what anybody says, the money trail led to Hauptmann."

Haines launched into the story.

"I left Hopewell and returned to New York right after the Lindberghs returned to Englewood. Around the same time, the Jersey State Police were taking a lot of heat. The baby was dead, the ransom payment was made, and a Lindbergh maid named Violet Sharpe, who may have been linked to the kidnappers, killed herself by drinking a bleach concoction after a particularly hamhanded interrogation by Schwarzkopf's boys.

"Everybody was getting impatient. Lindbergh, Hoover, Fiorello LaGuardia—even FDR. Jersey had jurisdiction, all right, but everyone wanted the more sophisticated NYPD to take over."

There was federal involvement already, Haines explained. The ransom bundle Lindbergh delivered to The Bronx before the baby's body was discovered was packed by the IRS and loaded with gold seal bills. Gold seals guaranteed a U.S. dollar's value in gold. The country was going from gold standard to trust standard soon, and the government was going to call in all gold seal bills. Those who kept them could spend them, but they would stand out. The IRS recorded the serial numbers of every bill in the ransom package—over five thousand in all—and printed a thick booklet of the numbers and distributed them to banks nationwide. It wasn't long after the ransom drop that gold seal bills started popping up in New York City grocery stores and gas stations. The first bank to get a ransom bill was East River Savings, way uptown.

Haines knew a detective on the case named James Finn, a quiet, bookish Irish bachelor nearing retirement age, who tracked the smattering of ransom bills floating around. Haines described the big city map on Finn's office wall, marked with pins where each bill surfaced. Red pins for twenties, green for tens, black for fives. There was a heavy concentration of pins—mostly black—sticking in the Upper East Side, especially Yorkville, the American launching point for German immigrants after World War I.

Language experts thought the ransom note, with its pigeon-English misspellings, was written by a German, and the man at the cemetery ransom drop had a German accent.

Finn was also getting steady, reliable descriptions. Time after time, the billdropper was described as swarthy, with beady eyes, a large, thin nose, and a strong jaw. He was short and solidly built; a workman.

"In other words, he was a paint-by-numbers Bruno Richard Hauptmann, just waiting to be colored in," Haines said.

"Finn chased the money for more than two years. Sometimes the trail went cold because bank tellers got bored poring over the IRS booklet. When the Lindberghs offered a two-dollar reward for every bill turned in, the trail picked up again.

"Finn was relentless, but there were times the cops were just plain stupid. For instance, everyone knew May 1, 1933, was the national deadline for exchanging gold seal bills for standard greenbacks. You'd think police would post an undercover cop in every major bank. Hah! On that very morning, a short, stocky German immigrant walked into a Manhattan bank and exchanged almost $3,000 of Lindbergh ransom money. Finn was livid. Now the kidnapper had $3,000 of walking around money, meaning the gold seal trail would dry up for a while.

"Finn was right. It wasn't until November that someone dropped a five-dollar gold seal at a movie theater in Greenwich Village. The movie? *Broadway Through a Keyhole* written by none other than Walt Winchell!"

Haines said the theater drop started a string over the next year.

"Finn showed me his board filled with green and black pins and told me the kidnapper had spent most of the fives and tens in the ransom bundle. 'When he starts spending those twenties, we'll nab him.' Remember, in those days, we were still in the Depression, and dropping a twenty was like flashing a hundred today—it got people's attention. Surely some salesgirl or female bank teller was going to take a longer look at Mr. Big Spender.

"Again, Finn was right. By the spring of '34, two full years after the baby was kidnapped, twenties started showing up.

"*East Side, West Side, all around the town ...*" Haines said. "By summer, the ransom bills were flowing like beer at a Bund rally, and it was mostly being spent in the German neighborhoods uptown and in the Bronx. Whoever was spending was getting comfortable, or he was tired of traveling to cover his tracks, Finn figured. Either way, the noose was tightening."

Finn and Haines had a deal. Haines would keep the progress out of the paper—"Finn didn't want to scare the guy off"—and Haines would get an exclusive on the "hero cop who broke the case."

Haines went with Finn to banks, gas stations, and restaurants to ask tellers, attendants, and waiters to be on the lookout. "If you get one of these," Finn would say, showing them a gold seal bill, "write down whatever you can about the person in the margin—what they look like, their license plate, the color of the suit they're wearing—and call me right away."

Finn told Haines, "We're getting close. It could be any day. And you'll be the first to know."

"My reporter's nose told me the big story was about to break and I was ready," Haines said. "My blood was pumping and I was sleeping light, waiting for that middle-of-the-night call from Finn. Some nights, while drifting in and out of sleep, I could almost hear his voice saying, 'Haines? It's Finn. We got him.'"

One night in early September, Haines's phone did ring. It was after 3 AM, and Haines expected it to be Finn, but it was Dicks.

"He told me to grab Max and get to Jersey. A luxury ocean liner called the *Morro Castle* was burning off the coast.

"I said, 'Don't send me down there. Not now, with the Lindbergh case about to break. The cops have traced the money all over uptown and the Bronx—my informant says they're ready to move in.'

"Dicks asked for the details and like an idiot, I gave him everything," Haines said. "Finn, his pin board, the German connections. I thought I could convince him to keep me close. Instead it had the opposite effect. Once I gave him the precious details, he could scuttle me to Jersey and hand my story to Winchell.

"When I was done, all Dicks said was, 'Listen Haines, if you like working at the *Mirror*, you'll come grab Max, then get your ass to Jersey and cover this ocean liner thing.'"

Haines was there the day the liner burned, but I knew the story inside out as well. Every decade brought another anniversary and a dwindling list of survivors and rescuers. After so many years at the *Shore Record*, I had written my share of *Morro Castle* stories. In fact, I'd long considered writing a novel about it, using the ship as a metaphor for the recklessness that led to the Great Depression. It was a story of abandoned stewardship and capitalist greed, spending frivolity, pervasive debauchery, and U.S. imperialism. You know what they say: the more things change ... I thought it could be my break-out book, the Great American Novel. I did a few chapter outlines, here and there, but, like Haines, never sat still long enough to write it. News got in the way.

The story in a nutshell was this:

The *Morro Castle* took passengers on a round trip from New York to Havana, which became known as the "Whoopee Cruise" in the years of Prohibition. It was a week-long party for passengers, but for New York waterfront gangsters and their associates in Cuba, it was a smuggling operation. The Ward Line, which owned the ship, paid its staff far less than any other and got what they paid for: pirates in starched uniforms. The crew was controlled by the emerging Italian Mafia, which traded jobs for cash then got a percentage of the swag: Cuban rum, Canadian whiskey, opium, heroin, gaming tables, Chinese laborers, Brazilian prostitutes. The most famous illegal import the *Morro Castle* ever carried was General Julio Herrera, who paid $5,000 in Yankee dollars to escape Cuban dictator Gerardo Machado, who'd put a price on his head.

In the ship's dining halls, bars, and lounges, booze flowed. Behind cabin doors, narcotics and marijuana came out and clothes came off. I heard stories of orgies in state rooms. Wife-swapping, wives performing, cabin boys being paid to service

Missus or Mister, or to stand by and watch. Maybe these were just stories, but silent porno films from South America were smuggled onto the ship, which carried a dozen small projectors.

When the week was over, the passengers staggered off the ship on Saturday, nursed their hangovers, and by Sunday were upright in church pews back home in Larchmont or Greenwich or the Upper East Side.

The FBI was battling waterfront mobsters, and J. Edgar Hoover himself warned Ward Line executives to clean up the ship. They were forced to hire a squared-away captain named Robert R. Wilmott, who promised to run the "Moral Castle." The first thing he did was forbid fraternization between crew and passengers— SOP on other lines. He held captain's inspections, personally covering every inch of the ship before it left New York, and again when it left Havana. He would dump overboard whatever he found. Bags of marijuana and barrels of rum went into the harbor. One trip he broke up a smuggled roulette table with an ax. On another, he turned a half-dozen political stowaways over to the Cuban police.

With their illicit incomes dried up, the crew grew mutinous. They refused to do basic maintenance or routine drills and complained about the lousy grub after Wilmott stopped feeding them from the passenger's galley. One boilerman confronted the captain on the bridge with a plate of runny eggs and watery grits.

"I wouldn't feed this to my dog," he said.

"Your dog isn't under my command!" the captain bellowed.

Tensions aboard the ship grew "thick as Sandy Hook fog and explosive as the *Lusitania*," an old first mate told me. Wilmott didn't trust anybody. His nightly dinners with passengers turned into inquisitions about late night parties, and his dealings with crew lurched between Captain Bligh tyranny and Hamlet paranoia.

The stress gave him heart palpitations. "You could see his carotid artery jitterbugging in his neck when he got angry," the first mate said.

The ship caught fire around 3 AM on September 8, 1934, hours after Wilmott died in his cabin.

After a day of ferreting out swag, Wilmott was exhausted and became ill. As the ship dove and rolled through gale force winds off the Carolinas and Delmarva Peninsula, he lay in his cabin. Instead of dining with passengers, he ordered a steak from the galley, blood-red. At about 7 PM, he called for the ship's doctor, complaining of constipation and severe heartburn. By the time the doctor got there, he was dead. The doctor pronounced it a heart attack. But when word circulated through the crew, an undercurrent of congratulatory glee made some officers wonder if the captain had been poisoned. Arsenic was in no short supply, used to kill rats. The doctor himself summed up these misgivings. In his farewell toast to the expired captain with the other officers, he said, "Here's to death. Which one of us will be next?"

Wilmott's death left Chief Mate William Warms in charge. Warms had been at the helm, but with Wilmott dead he decided on a more direct route home. Instead of skirting the storm, he took the ship through the heart of it. "The wind howled like Hell's ghosts, and high seas washed over the bow," the old mate told me.

The fire broke out in a blanket room then spread to the writing room, where Persian rugs, silk-lined curtains, and overstuffed upholstered couches burned hot enough to buckle the steel ceiling and deck above. Warms was unfamiliar with the fire hydrant system, and after he ordered all spigots opened, water pressure was lost in the pipes closest to the blaze, and the storm gusts whipped up the flames like bellows. He took the ship due east, planning to beach it. Panicked crew members failed to shut hatches as they fled rather than fighting the fire. The ship was full aflame and without power as the lights of Jersey's coast came into view.

When the order came to abandon ship, there was nothing but chaos. Lifeboats were dropped into the water half-full. A few got tangled in lines and dumped passengers into the ocean on the way down. More than half never got launched at all. The crew began to save itself; of the 85 people who made it ashore in lifeboats, almost all were crew members. As the fire and chaos spread, passengers were faced with two choices: jump or burn. They went over the side like lemmings, and 137 died. Some drowned; some broke their necks in the fall, when their life-preservers snapped up on impact, like a hangman's noose.

An investigation into the fire and behavior of the crew led to indictments of Ward Line executives, Warms, and the chief engineer, and to widespread safety reforms in the industry.

Those are the facts. But the mystery remains. Was Wilmott murdered? Was the fire intentionally set?

Anything close to an answer would only come years later, in the crazy case of George Rogers, the radioman aboard the *Morro Castle*. Rogers had long been regarded as one of the heroes of the night. He stayed at his post as other crew jumped ship and tapped out SOS signals hundreds of times, sending the message of distress into the empty night. When the transmitter batteries blew, Rogers was sprayed with sulfuric acid, but still managed to hook up the emergency unit. When the cables came unhooked, he fixed them with his bare hands and was shocked and burned for his effort. He was the last crew member to leave the ship and was lauded as a hero.

But Roger's story turned bizarre after he left the Ward Line. He opened a radio repair shop in Bayonne, which burned down. When he got a dispatch job with the Bayonne Police Department, he sent an incendiary device to a superior who thought Rogers was a pyromaniac and a paranoid nut and wanted him fired. The man was badly burned, and Rogers went to jail. After his release, he bludgeoned a neighbor and his adult daughter to death when the man asked him to repay a loan. The hero of the *Morro Castle* was, in fact, a sociopath who, starting as a teenager, drifted from job to job, leaving fires and assaults behind him. He was convicted of the double homicide in 1954 and died in prison.

I told all this to Haines, who nodded along as we crossed into Spring Lake, passing through the two stone roadside gates where Ocean Avenue became exclusively residential. The homes—mansions, really—spanned a century of great wealth: rambling Victorian-era sea cottages with turret roofs and multiple gables built by early industrialists; Craftsman- and Tudor-style houses built in the 1920s by New York law partners and advertising men; stone Italianate monstrosities built by modern Wall Streeters.

At the first mention of George Rogers, Haines blurted, "Oh, yeah—Fat Boy! I know all about him. Hell, I *created* him! The lone shining moment in his miserable life started with a newspaper article titled KINGS OF THE CASTLE, by Yours Truly. I thought he was the big hero of the day, and, oh, what a comedy of errors followed. Years later, when his defense attorney tried to submit that tissue of lies as evidence of his fine character in the Bayonne trial, the judge was indignant. He said, 'I daresay a story from the *New York Daily Mirror* cannot be viewed as valid, credible, or admissible evidence.' Boy, oh boy, did he get that one right!"

"Why 'Fat Boy'?" I asked.

"That's what the captain called him," Haines said. "Wilmott hated him, and vice versa. I'll tell you all about it. But drive all the way down to the South End, by the big hotels."

For most of the 20th century, there were three giant luxury hotels along Ocean Avenue near the South End of Spring Lake. The Monmouth, whose red roof and domed cupola gave it a Vatican look; the Warren, which was styled after an English Tudor country manse; and the Essex & Sussex, a Georgian Colonial of antebellum appeal. Only the latter still stood, now converted to age-restricted condos.

At the South End, Haines had me park by the yellow-brick pavilion, accented by terra cotta tiles portraying sailboats, seahorses, and other nautical images.

"This wasn't here when the *Castle* burned," Haines said. "It was added during the WPA years, a project for masons and ceramic artists."

I helped him into the wheelchair and pushed him to the boardwalk, the wind at our backs. I turned in front of the pavilion, which blocked the wind and made the day quite comfortable.

"This is where I covered it," Haines said. "Just a couple weeks before Hauptmann got arrested, when Winchell and Dicks conspired to gyp me out of the Lindbergh story. But in the end, I learned more important lessons down here."

"Tell me," I said, but he needed no encouragement.

11

By this time in '34, Haines had his own car, a maroon Ford Model A with a dashboard radio. Within an hour of Dicks calling, he crossed into New Jersey, with a drunken Max riding shotgun.

"Maxie smelled like O'Casey's at closing and was yakking away like a Bensonhurst housewife. 'Me and you, together again, Haines-boy,' he said over and over. Don't remind me, I thought. I couldn't wait for him to pass out, which he finally did on Route 9 South, down in the Amboys.

"Route 9 was the only way to go in those days, all through the industrial corridor of Jersey, past the new Newark airport, where floodlights illuminated a fleet of shiny TWA prop planes called 'The Lindbergh Line,' past the Bayway oil refineries, where smokestacks that looked like giant cigarette lighters sent flames high in the sky and left the air smelling like rotten eggs. Near the concrete bridge over Raritan Bay, the chemical factories and power plants were all going full tilt in the night, lit up and smoking like the ocean liner I had to find burning somewhere off the coast."

On the other side of the bridge, the landscape changed, and the salty smell of briny water filled the air.

"I knew I was getting close to the shore as the road cut through towns of small bungalows, shot-and-beer joints, and cabin motels," Haines said. "Then I got a lucky break. Up ahead, I saw the flashing lights of an ambulance. Since it was now almost six in the morning—way past the time for drunks to be out wrecking cars—I figured they must be heading toward the shipwreck. As long as that ambulance headed south, I was going to follow it."

Haines tailed the ambulance for ten miles through the big resort towns of Long Branch and Asbury Park, with their first-class hotels, amusement piers, and carousel houses, into the more sedate seaside hamlets that dot the coastal map. That's when he first heard the air horn sirens wailing incessantly from town to town, a call for all volunteers to head to the beach.

"I saw an orangey ball glowing out over the ocean and thought it was the sunrise on the horizon breaking through the morning clouds," Haines said. "Then I noticed the sky was turning a lighter gray due east. *That* was the rather unspectacular sunrise. The orange glow was the *Morro Castle* burning just a mile off the coast right here."

Haines pointed south from his wheelchair, past one of the granite boulder jetties, the erosion barriers that ran one hundred yards out into the water. "Me and Max parked further up the beach. Down here was blocked off for ambulances and such.

"Back then, the town looked like something out of *The Great Gatsby*, with the mansions and block-long hotels protected from the ocean by grassy dunes. The big liner was about a mile out, a torch emerging from the horizon, and black smoke billowed from her stacks and decks. She was listing, angling toward shore, emerging from the mist like the ghost ship she was. We could see people jumping off her deck into the ocean, whipped up by a vicious southeasterly wind.

"The sight sobered Max right up. 'Jesus Christ,' he said in no more than a whisper. 'It's either burn or drown.' I scribbled the words in my notebook.

"We hopped off the boardwalk onto the sand. It was about a ten-foot drop, and Max landed bad, falling on top of his camera gear. We ran into the wind toward the ship, pulling our hats down tight. The gusts were warm but wet, and the sand being kicked up stung our faces. The rush of wind was the bass line to the shrill air horns, which were wailing like a thousand Sicilian widows, and the air was getting thick with oily smoke."

Haines saw an army of rescue men descend on the beach. Thirty men in T-shirts and white bathing suits worked frantically to anchor thick lifeline ropes to wood pilings driven into the sand. Another thirty stripped down to their underwear, getting ready to plunge. Eight-man crews pushed a dozen lifeguard skiffs into the surf. The strongest men rowed out, knifing the sharp bows of the skiffs through the rough waves. The men on shore roped themselves together in human chains to reach victims in the roiling surf.

"Me and Max got up close to the action, and he started snapping," Haines said. "One guy yelled, 'Hey you! Help or get out of the way!' Then the guy shoved Max, who backpedaled about five feet and went down. This was no small feat. Max was a chunky, thick-shouldered fella, and no slouch. And mean when drunk or sobering up. But these shore guys were all lean and athletic, with strong arms and shoulders built up from rowing and swimming through the surf. I got Max off his ass and told him it was best we stay out of the way."

Haines looked out over the ocean, then back to the beach. "One thing about life and death situations. They bring out the best and worst in people. I saw that on this beach. More important, I learned about the dignity that comes when a man exhausts himself trying his hardest, even if he can't save everybody. I was changing. Maybe it was the Lindbergh baby pictures and Sara's shaming of me, but I was losing my desire to trample people for a story. When the naked girl washed up, I knew I would never go back to the way I was."

Haines waved his arm in both directions over the beach.

"All up and down, it was a terrible scene of human suffering. Remember, this was the early '30s. In this part of the world, only war veterans, cops, and ambulance workers had seen such human carnage. There was no TV, or those crazy, gory movies they make these days. The sight of flowing blood and gaping wounds was alarming back then, as it goddamn well should be!"

I nodded, thinking about how we're bludgeoned with images of horror today. Violent movies and video games are blood-drenched, each new release presenting more realistic and inventive ways to decapitate and eviscerate than the last. Graphic television images, from earthquakes to suicide bombers, come to all of us, like it or not. We can't unplug. Life was so much more civil back in Haines's day, when a fuzzy black-and-white photo of a woman in the electric chair or a baby on a morgue slab was considered shocking and in bad taste. I said all this to Haines.

"You're right," he said. "I thought I was hardened, because I'd seen plenty of blood-splattered crime scenes. And maybe I was— what's the word?—*dehumanized* enough to go with Ruth Snyder or Little Unlucky. But the *Morro Castle* ..."

Struggling to retrieve a memory, he closed his eyes tightly for a few moments.

"People kept coming ashore, horribly burned, skin peeling in patches of charred black and blood red. Some were screaming in agony, others were utterly silent, in shock, the salt water on their raw flesh creating pain that can't be described. The lucky ones died. The unlucky ones hung on for days, even weeks, killed slowly by infection.

"In the waves I saw a drowned child, a little boy dressed in white sailor pajamas, being tossed in the surf like ... a mannequin of driftwood. I thought of Little Unlucky, and my knees gave out. This

kid, like all the dead ones, was face down, left to the tide as rescuers concentrated on the living. Then a wave deposited the body
on shore, not ten yards from me.

"I sat in the wet sand, unable to move. My face was soaked by
rain and salty from ocean spray, and I convinced myself I wasn't
crying. Max was screaming at me to get up, but I couldn't. It was all
too big, too big to write."

Haines was yanked to his feet by Max, who grabbed him by
both lapels and yelled, "Get a grip, Haines-boy!" before dragging
the unresponsive reporter a few yards down the beach. In the
water nearby, two lifeguards were swimming toward a flailing girl.
"One was the same guy who'd knocked Maxie on his ass—a big
broad-shouldered guy with a Gene Tunney haircut," Haines said.
"I'd never seen such a powerful stroke. He cut through those
swells like a German U-boat, chopping through the waves one
long arm at a time."

The lifeguard reached the girl and brought her in with a side
crawl. When they emerged from the murky green sea, Haines saw
the girl was naked, her clothing stripped off by the turbulent sea.
She was coughing and spitting up sea water.

"I heard Max say, 'Haines! Wouldja lookit that!' just like he did
when he saw Little Unlucky on the slab. 'Oh, baby! Showtime,
Haines-boy, just like you always say!'

"'Maxie, for chrissakes!' I said as I tried to stop him, but he ran
past me into the surf, knee deep to get closer. I saw him fumbling
with the Speed Graphic, trying to jam in a film plate. He couldn't
get the camera to work and was cussin' up a gale of his own. The
lifeguard dragged the girl past Max, and yelled, 'Somebody get
some blankets!' They splashed past Max, still fumbling with his

camera. 'Slow 'em up, Haines, slow 'em up!' he screamed. 'I almost got it!'

"The lifeguard called out to me, 'Hey, you, this girl is freezing—give her your coat, quick!' I didn't move. I couldn't move. 'Goddamn it, give her your coat!'

"Then I heard Max, again. 'Slow 'em up, Haines!'

"I did nothing, either way. The guard looked at me with the same pure hatred I'd seen in Schwarzkopf when I asked him about the wild animals, and Max cursed me as I stood there, frozen.

"By then, a man had jumped from the boardwalk, where blankets donated by town residents were coming in, and ran to the girl with a large down comforter. The man bundled her up and headed her to the pavilion.

"Max was livid. 'Ahh, Jesus Christ, Haines! I missed the shot!' He chased after them, and I trudged behind. He was hollering to the blanket guy, 'Hey, hold up! I wanna put you in the paper! Beach heroes and the girl they saved!' but a lifeguard blocked his path.

"'Beat it,' he said to Max.

"Max tried to get past him, but the guy stepped in his way. 'I said, beat it. There's people drowning out there.'

"'Look, just one picture,' Max said. 'Just turn her 'round. And lower the blanket off her shoulder a little. You know, show a little shoulder.'

"And that's when the lifeguard grabbed Max by both lapels and pushed him down hard. '*You* look, you rotten son of a bitch, that girl nearly drowned. Take one more step in her direction, and I'll show you how it feels.'

"Max was on his ass in the sand. He held up his hands. 'Take it easy, pal,' he said, 'Just trying to do my job.'

Haines shook his head. "*'Just trying to do my job.'* Can you imagine? The standard excuse for our intrusiveness, the old refrain. What kind of *idiot* says that to a guy whose job is saving lives? I felt embarrassed for both of us, and I was suddenly aware of how insignificant my own job was. I was there to cover a tragedy; the lifeguard was there to correct it. You tell me, which is more important?"

Haines asked me to wheel him down the boardwalk. "Let's go for a walk." He pulled his blanket up as I pushed him into the wind. He took deep breaths as if to bottle the salt air in his lungs to bring back to the nursing home and told me the rest of the story, shouting against the wind.

"I was overwhelmed by this sudden sense of uselessness, in the moment, yes, but also looking back over my whole career," he said.

He and Max left the beach, left the lifeguards to their work, and followed the ambulances to the Army Camp in Sea Girt. There, the barracks had been transformed into a makeshift hospital, morgue, and interrogation room for the crew. Despite his lost enthusiasm, Haines wandered between places to find a story.

"I had to piece it all together, dazed as I was," he said.

In the barrack where crew members were being questioned by police, an MP told Haines about "the two Georges."

George Rogers was the chief radioman, a heavy, six-foot-two sullen oddball, without a friend aboard, or anywhere else, it seemed. The radio room assistant was George Alagna, a high-strung and wiry guy, a vocal malcontent who was trying to unionize the ship's crew. Wilmott was suspicious of both men and wanted them fired. "Fat Boy and the Communist," was how he referred to them.

But on the night of the fire, the two Georges acted heroically. As the fire spread and the crew abandoned ship, the two Georges stayed in the radio room, pounding out distress signals. Everything was black around them, and they had to breathe through wet towels.

"The metal floor plates were so hot the rubber soles of their shoes were melting like chocolate on August asphalt," Haines said. "The heat was turning the radio room into a convection oven, and Fat Boy was the Christmas turkey, literally roasting in his own juices."

When the radio transmission lines were fried, Alagna raced to the smoldering deck to set off flares. The two Georges were the last crewmen aboard when the rescue ships finally arrived to take off the remaining passengers.

"I had to do something, so I made the two Georges the day's heroes," Haines said. "Even though my gut was screaming not to."

"Why is that?" I asked.

"When I interviewed 'Fat Boy,' I detected the evasive eye movement of a liar. I convinced myself he was simply being humble. Why? Because it fit my story. The Humble Hero. Alagna was even more squirrelly.

"I phoned Dicks with my 'exclusive'—that is, my exclusive bunch of baloney.

"He was ecstatic. 'This is a Page One extravaganza! You're a pain in the rear-end, Haines, but you do good work!'"

Max did a portrait of the two Georges, their faces black and purple with burns and soot, as they lay side-by-side on cots in the Sea Girt sick bay.

That picture ran under the next day's Page One headline that said, KINGS OF THE CASTLE: *HERO RADIOMEN SAVE HUNDREDS IN FIERY DISASTER AT SEA*.

The *Mirror* story made the two Georges instant celebrities. Other papers chased Haines's story, and Pathe newsreels did a feature shown in theaters across America. The two Georges were given a hero's welcome back in New York; LaGuardia handed them the keys to the city in a hugely attended ceremony outside city hall. And then they were forgotten, until George Rogers tried to blow up his Bayonne police supervisor, then later killed his neighbors. The hero of the Castle became the prime suspect, though nothing was ever proven.

***

"I didn't know Hauptmann's name the day the *Morro Castle* burned," Haines said, "but I knew he was lurking right around the corner, ready to be caught. And it was my story, or so I thought."

Haines and Max packed up and headed home. At some point, Haines turned on the car radio to divert his mind from the day's images.

"And it was right then I heard that irritating voice of Winchell's, such a big shot now with his own radio show, cracking through the static of some shore town NBC affiliate.

"'*Good Evening, Mr. and Mrs. America, and all the ships at sea ... Well, folks, there's one less ship at sea tonight. The 11,520-ton* Morro Castle, *the bawdy queen of the New York-to-Cuba fun run, or should I say rum run, burned today off the coast of the picturesque Jersey Shore ...*'

"Then the SOB proceeded to read *my* exclusive story of the two hero Georges almost word-for-word, like he was there. The guy who never got sand in his shoes, or his hair drenched, or smelled the burned flesh or saw the bloodless faces of the drowned, the guy who never left the cozy warmth of his studio at Rockefeller Center had all the details! I wanted to scream out to the world, 'Winchell's no reporter—he's a *radio actor*!'

"But then the real bomb hit ...

"'*Now we move to the BIGGEST news of the day ... New York City police are moving in on the Lindbergh baby kidnapper. According to informed sources at the highest level of the investigation, the kidnapper is most probably a German handyman or carpenter living in the Yorkville section of the Upper East Side of Manhattan or in one of the German enclaves of The Bronx. These same police sources tell me the kidnapper has spent all but the twenty-dollar gold seal ransom bills, and that John Q. Public—yes, you out there—should be on the lookout for those bills. The police ask that all you gas station attendants, movie cashiers, waitresses, bank tellers, merchants, anybody out there who handles cash, be alert and diligent and help them catch this fiend!*'

"I couldn't believe my ears! *Informed sources?* The source was *me*! Dicks gave Winchell *my* story, to blab to the world. I had a deal with Finn to keep the money thing quiet, and here was Winchell telling everybody! Worse, it turned out Finn wasn't mad, he was ecstatic. He attached himself to Winchell's star and began tipping him instead of me."

A few days later, a gas station attendant got a gold seal bill from a customer, and he wrote down the license plate and a description of the car and driver. The 1930 dark blue Dodge sedan was owned by B. Richard Hauptmann, who was arrested the next day at his home in The Bronx. Winchell broke the story on radio, making a special mid-day "Bulletin" appearance.

"Finn gave it all to Winchell. In the bulletin, Winchell gushed, '*Hauptmann was apprehended due to the relentless and exhaustive police work by one Detective James Finn, the finest of New York's City's finest, the man who single-handedly cracked the case. America salutes you, Detective Finn, for apprehending this fiend.*' If that wasn't bad enough, Finn credited Winchell for cracking the case in a Pathe newsreel, standing there with Winchell and the gas station guy.

"'*If Walt Winchell hadn't made that broadcast imploring people to be on the alert, this never would have happened,*' Finn said on the newsreel. '*It was Walt Winchell's broad appeal that gave us the break we needed.*'

"It was all a big lie," Haines said. "I'd been to that very same gas station, on 127th and Lexington, with Finn a few weeks earlier. I saw Finn tell the attendant, a big-eared guy named Walt Lyle, to be on the lookout for the bills. But now, on the newsreel, the three heroes were standing and smiling, nodding away like bobble-head dolls.

"I didn't realize it till years later, but it was the beginning of the end for us newspaper guys. Radio could instantly and cheaply reach millions of people without printing or delivering a sheet of paper. TV was coming. People no longer had to read, which required concentration. They just had to sit there and listen. The newspaper, the way I knew it, had seen its day."

12

It was also the beginning of the end for Fred Haines as a newspaperman. Back in New York, he threw a fit about how Dicks stole his story and gave it Winchell. Two days later, Dicks called him in. "Haines, you did so well on the *Morro Castle* that we're making you our Jersey correspondent," he said. "Permanently."

"Well, hell. I knew what Dicks was doing," Haines told me. "A handshake up front, a knife in the back. It was a demotion. A kick-aside. He might as well have sent me to Mars. Most of Jersey was boonies in those days, where I would wander like an outcast looking for stories."

Haines would assist Winchell at Hauptmann's trial, and hear, but not print, Bruno's confession. Mostly, he would cover sporadic crimes and call in "a few inches for the back pages."

The *Mirror* set him up in an office with a Murphy bed over in Perth Amboy, across the Arthur Kill from the first layers of New York City trash at Fresh Kills dump on Staten Island.

"At first I thought I was in newspaper limbo. There was no action, except maybe a chemical blast now and then. But after a while, I began to appreciate the pace. All those years of running, and now I had nowhere to go. So I stopped and took a look 'round and saw this."

He waved his hand over the expanse of ocean in front of us.

"I bought myself a little seaside bungalow down Highway 36 in the Atlantic Highlands, over top of Sandy Hook. On clear days, I had a panoramic view of my former world-at-large, Manhattan Island to Coney Island. Mornings, I'd sit on my porch with a cup of joe and watch the freighters come and go. On warm evenings, I would sit outside with a cigar and a scotch or two and watch the setting sun glint off the city skyscrapers, from the Woolworth Building up to the Empire State. At night, the distant carnival lights of the Wonder Wheel and Cyclone flickered high over the waterline.

"I'd watch giant oil tankers, flanked by Sandy Hook pilot tugs, move silently up-bay toward the Amboy refineries. I'd watch rickety fishing boats, two-piston engines banging, chug out of the salty Jersey bayside village of Belford. In summer, a flotilla of bright white sails would set out each morning, bobbing on the bright, blue water. Then I'd watch them return with the on-shore cool breezes, through the light fog of evening when the sea looked muddy green. In winter, there were enough stars out to confuse Galileo, and the autumn nor'easters and summer gales whipped up waves that would have scared Columbus.

"Against this backdrop, I numbed myself over what had happened in Hopewell with Sara. I began to care less and less about the newspaper, where work was steady and mundane but unimportant to me after the Hauptmann trial. I filed a couple of brief stories a day—mysterious deaths, fatal car accidents, house fires. Some made the paper, and some wound up on the composing room floor. Didn't matter much to me. Whatever they did to my stories at the paper, I always had that view and a bottle of Dewar's to keep me company.

"But one thing about news. It keeps coming ..."

***

In the mid-1930s, Haines's panorama included fly-overs by transatlantic airships. The docking station for New York was at the Naval Air Station in Lakehurst, a town in the Jersey pines where the Navy built a dirigible hangar big enough to house the luxury liners.

The hangar is still there, the length of three football fields, the width of two, and high enough to stand one up in. It is a Jersey engineering wonder; the Pulaski skyway of buildings. It is miles of steel girders and bands, and several tons of bolts and rivets, all connected in intricate patterns of age-proof stability and use.

Haines told me he wanted to see it one more time.

"It's not far from here. Let's take a ride."

I wheeled him to the car, and he hoisted himself in. Once the chair was folded, we were on our way, away from the Oceanview, out of Bradley Beach, through Sea Girt, then Brielle and Manasquan. Jersey Shore towns are a collection of poetic, rhythmic names; Victorian hamlets of seaside resorts. Absecon, Barnegat Light, Brigantine, Lavallette, Loveladies, Mantoloking, Margate, Mystic Island, Normandy Beach. Slightly inland, the terrain is sandy and dwarf-pined, and township names are plain and angular. Wall, Brick, Howell, Jackson. We drove inland on Highway 70, a flat straightaway through scrub pines, slowed only by senior citizens who live in the sprawling retirement communities of Leisure Village, Leisure Village II, and Holiday City.

Haines looked out the car window at the proliferation of strip malls, each anchored by a chain pharmacy.

"Last time I was here, there was nothing on the ground but pine needles. Pine cones and pine needles."

Hangar No. 1 at Lakehurst is the tallest building in the Pine Barrens; it's been that way since it was built in 1921. Over one rare mild elevation on the road, we saw it rise, almost 300 feet over the stumpy forest, like a refrigerator box tossed on an uncut lawn.

"There it is," I said to Haines, then realized ...

"Can't see that far," he said.

"We'll get there soon enough."

With that cue, Haines rolled out his story.

***

"It was a warm spring evening, the kind where the air is thick with a metallic smell. I was on my porch with a drink and a smoke when I saw a silver glimmer in the gray sky. I knew it was a Zeppelin, or the *Los Angeles* or *Akron*, which were two American blimps, 'cause they flew over all the time. I spent a good half-hour watching this one approach, like a perfectly shaped, silver storm cloud."

The airship route went over the south beaches of Sandy Hook. It didn't fly directly over Haines's head, but came close enough for him to see its name and the four-pronged polygon on the tail fins.

"I'd seen the *Hindenburg* before, but it was first time she wore Nazi swastikas," Haines said. "Remember, this was 1937, so I didn't think much of it. Mostly, I remember the temperature dropping soon after it flew over. Not like most spring evenings, but cold enough to force me inside."

A couple of hours later the Bakelite desk phone in Haines's bungalow rang. It was Dicks.

"Ever hear of the *Hindenburg*?" he asked.

"It flew over my house two hours ago," Haines said.

"Well, it ain't flying now. It just blew up in a place called Lakehurst."

Haines had no idea where Lakehurst was, except south, so he drove out to Route 9.

"No sooner had I got on the highway when two ambulances came up behind me. I let them pass, then tailed them," he said. "They were South Amboy crews, and others came in as we headed south—Asbury, Belmar, Spring Lake, Lakewood, and every other town along the way. It was a procession; a speeding Fireman's Fair parade."

Haines stayed in the ambulance pack and was waved through by Shore Patrol guards at the gate.

"When I got to Lakehurst, the *Hindenburg* was a smoldering bag of metal bones," he recalled. "Its eight-hundred-foot long frame was broken and twisted, rising like a burned bridge from a large, smoking puddle of black rubble on the Lakehurst tarmac."

He stopped and removed his glasses, cleaning each lens with his scarf ends. "That was some day," he said.

We were now close to the base, and I found the main entrance. I explained the situation to the Navy guard who stopped us. We were in luck, he said. The hangar doors, which were as heavy as battleships and glided over fortified railroad tracks, were open to let the hangar air out. We drove to it, and I unloaded Haines and his chair. I pushed him into the hangar, past a monument near the east door to commemorate the *Hindenburg* crash and honor its dead.

"This was the triage room," Haines said, as we looked inside the vast space. It was empty, used for occasional aircraft maintenance, but standing now only for the sake of its own history: an architectural marvel made most famous by an incendiary tragedy.

"Every doctor, nurse, and ambulance man in the area was here, trying to ease the pain of passengers and docking crew burned by the flaming hydrogen and the debris that rained on them when the ship exploded. The smell of burned flesh permeated the air— that's a smell I'll never forget.

"It was bedlam in here. It was dark, lit only by portable emergency lanterns. The shouts and screams of emergency workers and burn victims echoed off the walls until it was impossible to tell which was which. Add the piercing sound of sirens as ambulances arrived and departed, and you had a *blitzkrieg* of black noise.

"In one corner, there were fifteen or so bodies on stretchers, covered with sheets, leaching blood. I staggered through the area, taking notes. I remember writing the words '*a carnival of carnage*' and being immediately repulsed by my own trite image. I tried to talk to some of the injured, to get eyewitness accounts, but I was shooed away by an ambulance driver.

"I remembered the guy on the beach during the *Castle* rescue— the guy who said, 'Help or get the hell out of the way'—and I decided to write about the people who were helping here. I knew the best way to tell their story was to experience it."

So Haines ditched his overcoat and suit jacket and rolled up his sleeves. He saw a petite nurse struggling to steer a gurney with a moaning sailor on it. He got on the other end. He found crew still taking victims off the airfield by canvas stretcher and moved "15, maybe 20 people" from tarmac to triage center. He saw charred bodies, still smoking in the chilly night air.

"Get the living inside," an ambulance man told him. "Leave the rest for later."

When the survivors were all moved, Haines trawled the medical areas. Without being asked, he put on sterile gloves and opened packets of greasy bandages to protect the flesh of people with third-degree burns. He heard cries in German and English, the whimpering of burned women and men alike. He saw people exhaling black air from their charred lungs, a few breaths from death. He saw sheets pulled over heads, as doctors moved from the expired to those for whom there was still some hope. He helped carry the dead to the morgue area and the living to ambulances. He rode to a hospital in Toms River, then raced back.

"It went on like that for hours," he said. "I lost track of the time, but I knew I'd blown deadline. For once I really didn't care. My back and arms ached, my clothes were soaked in sweat. In the midst of all that misery, I felt ... I don't know, *satisfied*. Good inside. For the first time in my life, I was part of something, not just working the edges."

When he finally got around to calling the paper, he got Dicks.

"Where the hell have you been, Haines? We had to use wire service for the first edition!"

"I'm here ... at the scene," Haines said. "It was hard finding a phone."

"So now you got one. What have you got?"

Haines gave him known details of the crash; the suspected lightning strike or static electricity build-up that ignited the hydrogen. He told him the number of dead, the who's who among the passengers, then concentrated on the heroic actions of the medical people and rescue squads.

"Never mind all that," Dicks said. "What about the Nazis?"

William Randolph Hearst, to whom Haines mockingly referred as Wilhelm Adolf Hearst, was known as a "Nazi sympathizer," a term made popular by Holocaust investigators. Lindbergh was another. Lindy had toured Germany's aircraft factories and come away awed by the nation's industrial advances and potential military might. Hearst visited, too. As early as 1934, he luxuriated in the famous mineral baths at Bad Nauheim, then met Hitler in Berlin. Like Lindbergh, he was guided through Hitler's factories, including the Graf Zeppelin works at Friedrichshafen. But Hearst was more than a walk-about tourist. As Hitler's war machine ramped up, the U.S. ambassador to Germany, William Dodd, brought forward evidence that Hearst was a paid Nazi propagandist. He took a half-million a year from Hitler's party and in exchange gave them favorable press. From 1934 until Hitler's tanks rolled into Poland in 1939, the Hearst news entities ignored the storm clouds building over Europe, reporting only on Germany's economic gains and its peaceful ambitions.

"What Nazis?" Haines asked Dicks. "Nobody said anything about Nazis."

Dicks lowered his voice. "I'm told there were Nazis on board making a goodwill trip to the United States."

"Who says?" Haines asked.

"An emissary from Mr. Hearst."

"Emissary, my ass!" Haines told me, retelling the story. "I knew what was going on. Hearst wanted to make it look like sabotage, as if the Nazis were victims! I said to Dicks, 'Well, I don't know nothing about no Nazis. Maybe I should talk to the emissary.' I thought that would be the end of it, figured there *was* no goddamn emissary, but instead Dicks said, 'Hold on.'

"Next thing I heard was a man who introduced himself only as 'Mr. Kriemer.' I detected a hint of German accent, though nowhere as thick as Hauptmann's.

"Kriemer suggested, strongly I might add, that anti-Nazi fervor was behind the crash. He said he had information that a team of American Zionist assassins brought down the *Hindenburg* with an incendiary bullet. He had details. Said they were four Jews from New York, driving a black sedan, who shot from a deserted Pine Barrens road less than a half-mile from the hangar.

"'That's funny,' I said. 'The hangar's in the middle of the base, a mile in. And the base is barb-wired all around. Besides, you know

how four New York Jews in a black sedan would stick out down
here with these Pineys?'

"Kriemer suggested the men 'may or may not' have been let
onto the base. I countered that the Navy ran a tight ship. Kriemer
then said 'it was curious' that the United States Congress had
recently banned the sale of helium to Germany, forcing the
Hindenburg to fly on hydrogen, which is much more flammable
and explosive. He hinted at a high-level conspiracy.

"'Are you saying our government took it down? That's nuts,' I
said. 'This is sounding a lot like *Remember the Maine!* except Mr.
Hearst is on the wrong side.'

"'On the contrary,' Kriemer said. 'Mr. Hearst doesn't want
un-American influences in this country to lead us into war with
Germany.'

"My head was spinning. Nazis. Zionists. Murder and sabotage.
Hearst and my paper in the middle of all of it. The world about to
spin out of control. All it needed was a little push, a little inflam-
matory story here, a rabid editorial there.

"'Maybe it was just an accident,' I said. And you know what he
said back? 'There are no such things as accidents on the international level, Mr. Haines. Nothing happens in a vacuum. Mr. Hearst
himself suggests you take that line of questioning down there.'"

Haines went back to the hangar and found several surviving
crew members. They spoke no English, but the captain, Max
Pruss, through an American engineer who spoke German, told
Haines he thought static electricity from an oncoming storm had
ignited the volatile hydrogen. U.S. Navy dirigible experts said the
same thing.

Haines asked if anybody had heard a shot.

"They looked at me like I was crazy."

Relieved, he called Dicks.

"'No conspiracy, and no incendiary bullet,' I told him. 'It was static electricity.'

"'We'll see about that,' Dicks said, and hung up on me."

When Haines picked up the paper the next day, he didn't recognize his story.

The giant dirigible *Hindenburg*, the pride of the German Zeppelin fleet, mysteriously exploded while docking at Lakehurst, New Jersey, killing 36 people, including at least nine goodwill ambassadors from the reigning political party of Adolf Hitler.

U.S. Navy investigators, who asked that their names not be used because of the delicate nature of their probe, said the airborne luxury liner may have been brought down by incendiary bullets that ignited the millions of cubic feet of hydrogen gas used to float the airship.

Witnesses said they heard the "pop" of what could have been gunfire, before the *Hindenburg* erupted in a ball of flames.

Investigators last night combed the pine tree woodlands around the Lakehurst air base, looking for evidence of the snipers, who caused so much death and agony, and may have done irreparable harm to the relations between two world powers.

Witnesses in the area, who asked to remain anonymous because they feared retribution, said four suspicious men in a black sedan with New York license plates were seen spying in the area with binoculars from a deserted pinelands road. The men, these witnesses said, were believed to be Jews.

In Berlin and Washington, officials were awaiting the results of the investigation, but sources say the German government is outraged that the United States failed to protect their transatlantic flagship from "Zionists, Communists and others who want to see the government of Hitler fail."

"It went on and on like that—propaganda worthy of Goebbels himself," Haines told me. "I called Dicks. 'Do you realize what you've done? The only incendiary bullet fired was the one by our paper. Think of the trouble this could cause.'

"'Hey, Haines, when did you become such a chicken liver?' Dicks said. 'And when the hell did you get a *conscience*?'

"'You can't just go making something like this up,' I said.

"'Why not?' he asked. 'Nobody takes this rag seriously. Don't you know that by now?'"

Haines looked around at me from his wheelchair.

"Funny thing was, I really didn't. Yeah, it was a big game to me for such a long time, but I also knew the power the paper had, rag or not. I saw the outrage when we printed the Lindbergh baby picture. I saw how my words swayed public opinion, making a hero out of a homicidal screwball like George Rogers. Sure, it was a rag, but people were moved by it and tended to believe what it said.

"I told Dicks, 'You're wrong. People do take it seriously. You don't see it because you're holed-up in the office, pretending to know everything, but I'm the guy out on the street. I'm the guy who knows the readers. You guys in the offices, you think the public wants all this blood and gore and controversy.'

"'They do,' Dicks responded.

"So I said, 'Yeah, well one day, they'll get sick of it. Then where will we be?'"

***

Fred Haines asked that question in 1937.

In 1999, when I interviewed him, the answer was apparent.

As you read this, the answer is emphatic.

Where we are is here.

My business is dying. The people who run it blame the internet and falling revenue. They sound like the American automakers in the 1980s and '90s who blamed the imports and labor, instead of admitting they got lazy and made an unreliable product.

So here we are, in the news business. Just as lazy, falling back on the old standbys like crime and tragedy, not realizing people feel bludgeoned by bad news. *Strike one.*

Lazy, too, on reporting "issues," becoming tools of political operatives and those invested in their causes. *Strike two.* The regular reader's voice is never represented. Here's something I believe: 95 percent of us want 95 percent of the same things. Economic opportunity. A decent education for our kids. Safe streets. Good medical care, God forbid we need it. Security, and to be left in peace to enjoy it.

Regular people aren't strident on issues, don't lean too far left or right. The common people have common sense, and a sense of common good. I think Americans, by their very nature, believe in fairness. It is the tree from which the branch of freedom sprang. Think about it. Think about our history. England was unfair. Slavery was unfair. Pearl Harbor, unfair. A free press was supposed to fight for that fairness—it's right there in the First Amendment. It was supposed to speak for the people, and therefore, speak to the people. (Read that "subscribers.") Speaking to the people is the only thing that could have kept news relevant.

For the years I was in the business, the news business missed this giant bullseye. News forgot or alienated the American middle class, the workaday, regular people. Instead, it spoke to, and spoke for, the people on the fringes. Those five percent, deeply entrenched in their issues, who believe the only fair thing is to have it their way. Every day, the rhetoric around abortion or guns or gays or race or the Religious Right or the Tea Party or the latest Washington sex scandal is as bludgeoning as daily crime. We have political polarization because journalists have become the tools of those who aim to politically polarize. Goodbye, integrity. I'm sad to admit this, but I think media is a destructive force in the country today. Instead of constructing dialogues about solutions, we play to ideology and fuel hysteria, just like old Hearst. We snipe, we take people down. We pull things apart, rather than push them together.

So here, instead, is what media companies have done with free press. Celebrity news. Reality TV. Singing and dancing competitions. Twenty-four hour sports. Shuck and jive.

"When celebrity replaces knowledge, there are grave implications for the future."

Strike three.

I said all this to Haines as I drove him back to the nursing home, glancing at him from time to time to make sure my pontification hadn't put him to sleep.

"You're a pretty smart fella," was all he said when I was done. "Now you get the picture. Jersey in the '30s."

It was twilight in the pines and dark by the time we got to the ocean.

"Drive up by the beach," he said. "I want to see it one last time."

He put down his window, and the night salt air rushed through the car. He poked his head out and looked up toward the stars he could no longer see.

13

When I returned Haines to Oceanview, "Bruno's Confession" was on his night table, waiting for me.

"Take it home and finish it. Then tell me what you think," he said.

We agreed to meet in a couple of days.

"If I'm still here," he chuckled. "At my age, I don't plan far ahead."

His dinner was brought to him, a thin-sliced meat of some sort with pasty mashed potatoes and gravy, julienne carrots, and banana pudding. He asked me to stay while he ate, but said little. When he finished, an aide came in and helped him out of his clothes and into bed.

"It's been a long day," he said. "A good one, though."

He removed his glasses, looked in my direction, and said, without pleading, "Stay awhile and read my book. Skip ahead to the trial. A lot of the other stuff I already told you."

I did, and read a bed-time story for Haines to myself.

Hauptmann's trial was set for January 2, 1935. Dicks sent me to down to Flemington to be Winchell's note-taker and quote-runner. It was bad enough they stole my story; now I was Winchell's caddie. Again.

And it was nauseating watching Winchell hold court each night at the Union Hotel bar, alternating between his stage-voice jokes and speaking with booming authority. He made it sound as if he'd been on the case from the very start, as I had. He pontificated and grandstanded like he was the star of the show, even though Damon Runyon and H. L. Mencken were there and could write figure-eights around him. I wanted to kick him in the ass again, but I knew I'd get fired. That, and he pretty much stayed far away from me at the bar, especially after I got a little snoot full.

It was Mencken who wrote that the trial was "the biggest story since the Resurrection," but I always thought he was being satirical. After all, the man covered World War I. Nonetheless, the Hauptmann trial did attract the world's attention like nothing before it. Reporters came from more than two hundred papers from both sides of the Atlantic. Bell Tel came and laid down a couple of hundred phone lines, making little Flemington, New Jersey, the most wired city on earth. Right across the street from the courthouse, the Union was booked full, with reporters doubling and tripling up in rooms. Every private home in town turned boarding house. Still, newsmen slept in cars and friendly saloons. For a buck a night, Flemington's lone pool room let guys bed down on felt-and-slate mattresses.

Me, I was lucky. Winchell wanted me close, so me and Max got to bunk together next to His Highness's private suite on the Union's third floor. We had one bed, so we took turns on the floor. Not that you could sleep. In the wee hours, just when the drunken reporters got done shouting and careening down the halls outside our door, the court spectators would start lining up on the street outside our window. Arguments and punch-ups were as regular as a milkman's rounds.

Hawkers wheeled souvenir carts filled with curly Q locks of blond hair like Little Unlucky's and "authentic" autographed pictures of the Lindberghs. Much to my disgust, reprints of my Mirror cover with the baby corpse were still selling like crazy.

The trial lasted 32 days but it seemed like half that. Everything moved so quickly because Judge Thomas W. Trenchard, up from Trenton, kept theatrics to a minimum. With all the press hyperbole, people anticipated a defense vs. prosecution showdown on the order of Louis vs. Schmeling, but the judge would have none of it. "Get to the point" and "Get to the question" were his two favorite directives.

When the Lindberghs took the stand, he was stoic and unshakable, she was nervous and emotional. The colonel held his own against Hauptmann's attorney, a New York sharpie named Edward Reilly, who kept hammering home his theory: "The maids did it." Reilly had the good sense to not cross-examine Mrs. Lindbergh, telling the court he didn't want to "exacerbate her grief," a rare time he won points with the jury.

Then came Dr. John F. Condon—"Jafsie," the cemetery bagman. Prosecutor David Wilentz, the Jersey attorney general, wanted him to identify Hauptmann as the man who took the ransom money. Condon had the spotlight and didn't want to give it up. He hemmed and hawed so much that Wilentz looked ready to strangle him.

Then there was Anna Hauptmann, Bruno's meek and homely soon-to-be-widow who concocted a flimsy alibi for her husband. Wilentz came down hard, and as she wept and twisted a hankie on the stand, she became as sympathetic as Mrs. Lindbergh herself.

Bruno was on the stand for three full days, taking rights-and-lefts from Wilentz, but remained strong-jawed about his innocence. Wilentz flipped every detail and tried to trip him up a hundred ways from Sunday, and still Bruno didn't budge. He came across just as everybody expected: a mechanical, unfeeling, defensive Kraut.

But there was one thing I noticed: Each time Wilentz began to make him sweat a little, Bruno would look at his wife, take a big swallow of air, then go back into his zombie act.

A parade of handwriting and currency experts were followed by a guy who traced the wood in the homemade ladder to a lumberyard near Hauptmann's home. None of it mattered. Hauptmann was guilty walking in and walking out. It was scripted that way. No one saw him near Hopewell. He never worked on the estate. Nobody ever linked him in any way to the Lindberghs. All prosecution had was the busted ladder, the ransom note, and the gold seal currency. And the universal motive of greed.

The jury began deliberations mid-morning on Wednesday, February 13, broke for lunch and dinner, and by 10:30 that night they had reached a verdict.

The horde of reporters nearly busted down the courtroom doors to get back inside. There was a public crush, too. The sheriffs let too many people in, and it was sardine-can, standing-room only. People shoved and shoe-horned their way into rows and the upstairs gallery. I was jammed in next to Winchell, of all people, smelling his hot, boozy breath; it was a chest-crushing crowd, and the temperature must have hit 100 degrees. I felt my knees go weak. The muscles in my thighs were involuntarily quivering, and I was sweating profusely, swampy in my suit.

The judge ordered the doors bolted and told the sheriffs not to let anyone out until it was over. He had the press searched for hidden newsreel cameras, and two Pathe guys got tossed. It took hell's eternity for the court to be secured. Finally, the jury was led in.

The crowd seemed to have one pulsating heartbeat. We knew we were about to witness a monumental news event, both historic and theatric. Trenchard banged the gavel asking for quiet in the court, but only when he began to speak did the place go dead silent. The judge addressed the jury, asking the foreman—a sinewy, no-nonsense Jersey hick named Charles Walton—if they had reached a verdict.

"Yes, we have, Your Honor," Walton said. "We find the defendant, Bruno Richard Hauptmann, guilty of murder in the first degree."

The place exploded before the "g" in guilty was out of his mouth. Winchell jumped and yelled, "I called it ... I called it," like he was the only one! The judge banged his gavel for order, and I yanked Winchell down by his overcoat.

"You're making a damn fool of yourself," I said. "And the rest of us, too!"

"I called it," he said again and again, until I put a hard squeeze on his arm.

"For chrissakes, shut up, Walt."

Trenchard kept banging, threatening to clear the courtroom, until he got order. When everybody was quiet, he pronounced the death sentence, which everybody knew was coming. Hauptmann stood in front of him expressionless, looking more dead than alive. Again the place exploded, and Trenchard went hard with the gavel, like a jockey whippin' his mount in the homestretch.

I kept my eyes on Mrs. Hauptmann, who sobbed openly, but quietly, with dignity. She never took her sad eyes off her husband, as if she wanted to soak up every last image of him to keep in the scrapbook of her memory.

Hauptmann, still blank-faced, was led out by a cadre of sheriffs. The jury was thanked and dismissed. Then the court was adjourned. Then all hell broke loose.

Outside was lit up like Times Square on New Year's Eve. Newsreel strobes and flashbulbs illuminated the crowd, which was packed shoulder-to-shoulder, from the front door of the courthouse to the hotel's front porch. To this day, I'm surprised no one suffocated in that crush, especially after some idiots started lighting bottle rockets and firecrackers in the throng.

Reporters and spectators mobbed the Lindberghs, Mrs. Hauptmann, and the attorneys as they tried to fight their way out. The Lindberghs had a phalanx of Jersey state troopers around them to beat the crowd back. One newsreel guy was laid out with the butt of a shotgun after he tried to break through to interview the Lindberghs. Meanwhile, poor Mrs. Hauptmann only had Reilly, her husband's attorney. They were soon overrun.

"Let the lady through! Have some decency!" I heard Reilly yell in his best courtroom baritone. Mrs. Hauptman was terrified. She must've been asking herself: Is this one of those notorious American lynch mobs?

I was still on the courthouse steps, caught in the crush, when I saw Reilly and Mrs. Hauptmann trying to fight their way back inside for safety. I muscled my way through the crowd toward them. The paper wanted fresh verdict reaction from Mrs. Hauptmann, but I wasn't interested in getting that. I wanted to rescue her. I failed. The crowd was too thick and unruly, and I couldn't push through. Reilly managed to enlist a few sheriffs from the courthouse steps to wade in and pull Mrs. Hauptmann out.

Those were the details I phoned in to the Mirror, *along with some perfunctory quotes from Reilly and Wilentz. By 3 AM, the party was still going strong, and I continued to call in man-on-the-street stuff and color from the scene. The next day's* Mirror *carried 32 pages devoted to the case, the trial, and reaction to the verdict. Twice as much as Armistice Day. Maybe Mencken was right. Winchell's column, full of my reporting, led the package.*

After my last dispatch to the rewrite man at the paper, I went to the hotel bar, which was open all night for the occasion, drained three straight-up double Scotches, bang-bang-bang, and, thanks to that, fell asleep on a lobby couch as the sun came up.

I looked up from the manuscript. Haines was asleep, still and flat on his back. His breaths were abrupt and sporadic. I watched for a few minutes to make sure they kept coming, turned off the reading lamp, and clicked on the night light next to his bed. I wondered how it felt to be a man Haines's age, knowing your adventures were numbered. I was glad I got the guy out and promised myself I'd do it again. I pulled the covers up and tucked them around his chin, leaned down and whispered, "See you tomorrow, Freddy."

I drove to Asbury Park and took a walk on the boardwalk from Convention Hall to the Carousel House and Casino and back. In 1999, the Asbury boardwalk was a mile of unfilled promise. Convention Hall was operational, but in disrepair, and the roof of the casino had caved in places. The Carousel House was rusted and boarded. But at night, when these great arcades weren't exposed to the truth of daylight, you could see the grandeur of their architecture. Jersey in the '30s, as Haines remembered it. I wanted to know more. At home, in my circa-1970s condo with all the design flourishes of a cinderblock Army barracks, I continued to read.

The next day, as I was packed to leave Flemington, a Hearst messenger stopped me. "New York wants you on the phone," he said.

It was Dicks. "Haines? We got a job for you ..."

Dicks told me a secret deal was cut for Hearst to buy Hauptmann's exclusive story after the verdict. Every tabloid in America was looking for the same thing, but old Hearst himself came up with a brilliant offer. Hearst knew Hauptmann didn't want his wife and toddler son to be left destitute, so he structured a deal to make Bruno a big winner if he was a loser—and an even bigger winner if he confessed to the paper. Midway through the trial, Hearst arranged a clandestine meeting with Reilly and made this sales pitch: Bruno's going to get convicted, or he's not. We want his exclusive story, either way. If he gets off, we'll pay him twenty-five thousand dollars for his story. But if he gets convicted, which means the electric chair, we'll pay him fifty thousand dollars. If he confesses to us, he'll get one hundred thousand.

Reilly said, why would he confess? He's innocent.

Hearst said, if he's convicted, it's academic. Whether he's guilty or not, he'll be dead, and his widow will be left a wealthy woman.

Of course, Reilly, too, would benefit. Hearst offered him a ten thousand dollar bonus to make it happen. Cash, of course.

No gold seal bills, Reilly said with a laugh as they shook on it.

"It's all arranged," Dicks told me that day on the phone. "You go in and ask him questions and write down the answers. It's his story, in his words."

"So now I'm Hauptmann's stenographer, too?" I said.

"Exactly," Dicks said.

"Get yourself another boy," I said.

"C'mon, Haines, it's the opportunity of a lifetime," Dicks cajoled. "You and Bruno, alone in his cell, yakking like a couple of schoolgirls at a slumber party. It'll be a great story."

"Forget it," I said. "I've had enough of this case."

I'd also had enough of the business; Mrs. Lindbergh's sorrow, Mrs. Hauptmann's fear, the Mirror *reprints of the dead baby everywhere I turned. Sara and my baby, just 10 miles down the road. All I wanted was to get out of Flemington as fast as possible.*

Dicks's tone hardened. "If you don't do it, you're fired."

"Fire me, then," I said.

"But if you do it, Mr. Hearst has authorized a five thousand dollar bonus for you. That is, if you get the confession."

At that moment, I saw myself taking Hearst's five thousand bucks with one hand and waving good-bye to his rag newspaper, Dicks, and Winchell with the other. A nest egg—that was the only reason I agreed to do it.

The deal called for Hauptmann to talk within a week of the trial's end, so I holed up at the Union waiting and watching as the town grew deserted.

One afternoon, with nothing to do but drink at the Union bar, my emotions got to me, three Scotches in. I called a cab and told the driver to take me out to Mount Airy. We drove down country roads to Aunt Margie's farm. The place was boarded up for winter. We drove to Hopewell, past Sara's father's house. Nothing much had changed.

"Just park here for awhile," I said.

"It's your nickel," he said.

After an hour, no one came or went, so we drove to Frelinger's. Another hour went by. The cabbie was first restless, now nervous. "This better be on the up and up," he said.

At six o'clock, the store lights and electric sign in front went off. It was dusk, and Jimmy Frelinger came out the front door, locked it behind him, and walked down the street.

"See that guy," I said to the cabbie, "follow him, but not too close."

"This better be on the level," he said. "I don't want no trouble."

I peeled a twenty from my billfold and dropped it over the seat. That shut him up.

Jimmy walked two blocks then turned on a street called Pierson Place. The houses were expensive on this side of town, big brick Federalists, with large windows. Jimmy turned up the walk of a cleanly trimmed brick home where the front porch and walk-way lights burned bright to welcome him.

   I had the cabbie pull over at the corner.

   "Wait for me here," I said.

   "Not without my fare so far," he said.

   I gave him another twenty.

   I walked to the house where Jimmy had turned. It was number 19. Later I wrote it down: 19 Pierson Place. Shrubs lined the walk and hugged part of the long porch. I moved in the shadows up the walkway and went around the side until I saw the family of three sitting down to Friday night dinner in a well-lit and well-decorated dining room. Sara looked lovely and content as she set a roasted chicken and bowl of rice and vegetables down in front of her husband. A curly-headed boy, just over two years old, sat in a high chair banging a spoon into some slop. The parents smiled at him, and Jimmy reached over and tousled his hair. I studied the boy's face, looking for some sign of me. And then I saw it. The pug face, the slit eyes. He was a Down syndrome child—what we called a "mongoloid" back then. My heart sank, and a sob came up. Anguished, is the best way to describe it. I had lost so much, but wrecked even more.

   Then I saw the way Jimmy loved that little boy, and I knew he did it better than I ever could. He fed him some, then wiped his face. He tickled him, made faces at him. The boy was laughing, happy; more than you could say for his father.

   I watched for a few minutes, standing in the cold, outside the warmth of their home. I told myself the tears running down my face were of happiness for her, for all of them. They had love and security. They had a life!

   I stayed until the cabbie tapped his horn. I didn't want him getting spooked and stranding me, so I took one last look over my

*shoulder, turned up my collar, and went back to the car. I never
saw any of them ever again.*

*I wrote her a letter in the 1940s, but never mailed it. My role
in her life was over. Now my role was to be forgotten, and remain
that way. My role was to protect our secret.*

*A day hasn't gone by that I haven't thought of her. Sometimes
she seems so real I can touch her. Other times, so abstract, I can't
believe she was ever real. Who was she? Did I really know her?
Did I really love her? Or did I create a fictional character out of
her, like I had done in so many newspaper stories? Sara, the lost
love. Lindbergh, the stoic, silent suffering hero. Hauptmann, the
dark, brooding, sinister criminal. Who were they really?*

*Her obituary gave some details. Her survivors, her civic life,
her commitment to the mentally retarded. Missing was the
essence of who she was, the way she looked and loved. Was she a
faithful wife? Was she a good mother? Did she sometimes stop
and think fondly of the man who clouded her past, who offered
her nebulous love but nothing concrete? Did her decision to end
that affair translate into happiness in her life? Did she die knowing she made the right choice, or were her final thoughts a series
of what-if regrets?*

*This is what I wanted to know. But she was dead, and I kept
living, such as it is.*

14

And what about Fred Haines? What was I to make of him? What would be *his* obituary headline, when the time came?

> FREDDY HAINES, LIVED 68 YEARS WITH A
>   BROKEN HEART
> FRED HAINES, TABLOID REPORTER, LINDBERGH
>   BABY PHOTO RUINED HIS LIFE
> FREDERICK G. HAINES, LAST OF THE YELLOW
>   JOURNALISTS

Our week of interviews was coming to an end; the manuscript was moving toward Bruno's confession. At some point, I had to put Haines in the newspaper. Would he be a paper-thin character? Of course I wanted to write a story filled with the different angles of one man who had lived a long and fascinating life. In the end, I wondered which side of Fred Haines would emerge from his house of mirrors as the dominant one. I kept reading.

On Saturday morning, a sheriff knocked on my door and handed me a note on the fancy, gold-embossed stationery of Edward J. Reilly, Esquire: "Mr. Bruno Richard Hauptmann, as agreed upon in a verbal contract with the Hearst Corporation, will be available for an interview today at noon."

I called Dicks and told him I was in.

"Get him to confess," he said, "and you'll have your biggest story ever."

"No kidding," I said. And my last, I thought.

Hauptmann had not confessed to the best of 'em. He stonewalled everybody, from heavy-handed Jersey state troopers to manipulative interrogators from the FBI and NYPD. He didn't confess to his own attorney, who could have helped him wiggle out of the murder charge and death sentence. If he'd admitted to the kidnapping, Reilly could have claimed the baby's death was a terrible accident, that Bruno's homemade ladder broke and he crushed the baby in the fall.

But I had two things none of Bruno's previous questioners had—a conviction, and a one hundred thousand dollar cash incentive. Now that he was sentenced to die, he might be ready to change his tune, for the good of his wife and baby.

In the courthouse basement, I was met by Reilly wearing a three-piece Prince of Wales plaid suit. His face was ruddy and swollen; bluish blood vessels road-mapped his cheeks, and the frames of his wire-rimmed glasses pressed the fleshy sides of his face. He looked like he'd been on a bender since the verdict.

"I'm Frederick G. Haines," I said.

"Yes, of course, the Hearst man from the New York Daily Mirror," he said.

We shook hands, and he took me aside. Not twenty-five feet away was Hauptmann's cell. A bored sheriff sat on a folding chair in front.

"Mr. Haines," Reilly began in a low, confidential voice, "I have the utmost respect for you gentlemen of the press, although, during the course of this ordeal, there have been a number of times in which I do not believe my client has been treated completely fairly. But this is neither here nor there. Water under the bridge, as they say.

"Now, sir, you have a unique opportunity, to come face-to-face with Mr. Hauptmann and hear his story, in his own words, exclusively for your ears, and, of course, the eyes of your readers. I will be present during this interview to guarantee the veracity of the statements attributed to Mr. Hauptmann, statements that will *appear in your fine newspaper and the other properties of the Hearst Corporation.*

"As you know, Mr. Haines, Mr. Hauptmann has been found guilty by a jury of his peers and sentenced to die by the swift and merciless hand of the State of New Jersey. I will not engage you again in the merits of the case. Suffice it to say, I do not believe due process has been followed and, therefore, justice may not have been served. An appeal is certainly warranted. However, the loss of this first round has been, shall I say, expensive and my client's resources have been quite depleted."

He held a beefy finger up to his lips and leaned closer to me. He was sweating, and I could smell the Irish whiskey leaking out of his pores and stinking up the worsted wool of his suit. He glanced toward the cell and lowered his voice another decibel.

"It's important we trust each other, vis-à-vis our arrangement," he said. "I've been assured you are a reasonable man, a man who knows how to play ball. So, confidentially, and I must trust your confidence in this matter, I should tell you I have begun quiet, but forthright, shall I say, negotiations with my courtroom adversary, Mr. David T. Wilentz, since the verdict was handed down. Mr. Wilentz, as Attorney General of the State of New Jersey, has suggested he may be amenable, perhaps even favorable, to a mutually beneficial arrangement in which all parties involved could avoid the somewhat messy and extremely costly business of a lengthy appeal process. As you know, the State's case is tenuous at best, and I don't think Mr. Wilentz wants to hold up his so-called hand-writing and police experts to further public scrutiny. I, on the other hand, am not in the business of pro bono representation, especially when the risk of coming out again, as they say, on the shit end of the stick is so great.

"Mr. Wilentz and I, therefore, have a mutual interest in striking a deal with Mr. Hauptmann that simply says this: The State

will spare his life if he were to simply confess to the kidnapping and the unfortunate, accidental death of the baby."

"So get him to confess," I said.

"Well, sir, it's not that simple," Reilly said. "Since the beginning of this case, Mr. Hauptmann has steadfastly, stubbornly maintained his innocence. When I spoke to him this morning about the deal Mr. Wilentz was considering, he refused to be party to it. 'Why should I confess when I am innocent?' he said. He then began peppering me about the prospects of success in the appellate courts, and I told him, honestly, they were not good. He has even refused Mr. Hearst's generous offer for simply murmuring the magic words, 'I did it.' 'But I didn't do it,' was his reply."

"Listen, get to the point," I said. I was growing tired of his sweaty, panting whispers. "What does this have to do with me?"

"Just this, Mr. Haines, just this. Mr. Hauptmann is very attached to his wife and little Manfred, whom he affectionately calls 'Bubi.' As you interview him today, I ask you to keep the line of questioning centered around his family. You know, leading questions, like, 'Do you think your wife will remarry after you are electrocuted?' 'Are you afraid of little Bubi being raised by a new man he will come to know as Daddy?' 'Aren't monthly visitations with your loved ones in prison better than being cast into the uncertain darkness of eternity?' You get the idea. Questions like these may get him to ask himself whether he is better off dead or alive.

"And, while you're at it, gently remind him that a soul-cleansing confession will redeem him in the eyes of his Christian God, while, in failing to confess, he condemns himself not only to death but to the blackness and lovelessness of hell."

"Take it easy," I said. "There's no jury here. Just me."

"Understood. I know it is in the best interest of the Hearst Corporation, the New York Daily Mirror, and—of course—you *personally, Mr. Haines, for you to get Mr. Hauptmann to confess. Between us—and I mean strictly between us—I have been offered a generous sweetener by Mr. Hearst to push Mr. Hauptmann in this direction. In that sense, Mr. Haines, we are partners, so to speak."*

I couldn't believe my ears.

"You're the poor bastard's lawyer, for chrissakes."

He again held his finger to his lips.

"Mr. Haines, please. I am his lawyer, true, sir. And as his lawyer, I must look out for the best interest of my client. And I can honestly—and ethically, too, I might add—say that it is now in Mr. Hauptmann's best interest to confess, so Mr. Wilentz and I, in concert, may spare what passes for his life."

"I'm going to go do my job," I said, flatly. "Whatever happens, happens. If he confesses, he confesses. If he doesn't, he doesn't. It's no skin off my nose."

"Please," Reilly said, mopping up his forehead with the folded silk hankie from his breast pocket. "Think of all the good it will do. Think of the Lindberghs, finally able to put this thing to rest. Think of Mrs. Hauptmann and little Manfred, with financial security and able to see their husband and father grow to old age. And think about yourself, I might add, a national hero for getting America's most despised man to finally confess, and richer for it, to boot!"

"And justice?" I said. "What about justice? Do you believe your client is guilty?"

"Rest assured, Mr. Haines. Justice will be served."

Then he led me to the cell.

John Steinbeck once said that journalism attracts the best of people and the worst of people. The worst are kingmakers and influence peddlers and pontificators. The best are people whose good intentions are to expose corruption and injustice, to fight for fairness in a world that tilts toward the powerful.

The best and worst. The same can be said for the world in which journalists work. In the court room, the battlefield, the political arena, there is good and not-so-good, if not evil. In his exchange with Reilly, I detected Haines's slight shift in integrity, drifting toward the better side. Not exactly noble, but tired of being a pawn in Hearst's game, and growing tired of manipulating hard facts into sensational stories.

Hauptmann's cell was surprisingly large. I had expected something no bigger than a horse stall, but it was the size of a parlor. Inside was a metal cot, chair, small reading table, and porcelain commode. Hauptmann was pacing, something he did often during our conversation.

During the trial, Hauptmann looked snappy every day in a charcoal double-breasted suit, his tie knotted in a perfect double-Windsor and a white handkerchief tucked neatly in his breast pocket. He was always impeccably groomed—hair trimmed, clean-shaven. Each day, he looked as though he came from the stock exchange rather than the stockade.

But now the show was over. In his cell, he had been stripped of anything he could hang himself with—necktie, shirtsleeves, belt, shoe laces. He wore a white T-shirt and a loose pair of old gray work pants. His shoes were battered, and he wore no socks. His beard, naturally heavy, was days old. Bruno the Bluebeard looked dangerous, a man capable of killing a baby. When I came in, he settled on the cot, and I sat in the chair. The room was painted battleship gray—floor, walls, and ceiling—and the jail bars black. When I think back on the scene now, I always see it as an old black-and-white movie.

I did not like Bruno Hauptmann. In court he came across as defensive and smug. He acted as if his arrest were some bad cosmic joke aimed at hapless him, an innocent man plucked from the crowd by fate. He played the victim, a man bullied by police, press, and prosecutors. He acted as if society had no right to ask how the Lindbergh ransom money ended up in his wife's pantry. I'd heard enough of his phony protestations in court, so I decided on a different tack in the jailhouse interview.

"Start at the beginning," I said. "Tell me about growing up in Germany."

"What? You don't want to know if I'm guilty?" he asked.

"I know you're guilty. The jury said so. That's how we do things in America," I said, to get his goat. "You say otherwise, and we'll get to that, but right now I want to hear about your early life."

"So, okay," Hauptmann said, and began to tell me his story. After five minutes, Reilly, looking as bored as the guard outside, looked at his pocket watch and said, "I have some business to attend to," then left. So much for guaranteeing the veracity of my report.

Hauptmann told me about his childhood in Krementz, which he made sound like a Saxony postcard: narrow streets lined with shops and row homes, a plain white Lutheran church perched above, all surrounded by hilly dairy farms. His family lived in a two-story stucco house at Bautzner Strasse 64. Bruno recalled how he ran lunch to his father at the quarry nearby, and sat with him and shared hunks of cheese, bread, and sausage.

"I was the baby of the family and my father's favorite. Those were very happy times for me. I was an innocent boy then. I had no idea of what life had in store for me."

In summertime, Bruno and his siblings—two brothers and a sister—would gather chamomile roots for tea and assorted berries for jams in the woods nearby.

"*My mother would always be cheerfully enthusiastic over our harvest, and I loved to do things that pleased her. Later, as we grew destitute, this desire to bring food to my mother would lead me down a different path.*"

The family became poor because Hauptmann's father was a drunk, and a mean one at that. He spent most nights at the local tap-haus, playing cards and darts in games where money changed hands. Mostly, money went from the father's hands into the hands of others; then hands clenched into fists. Bruno remembered his father cursing and spitting blood into the kitchen sink many nights. His mother would clean his cuts with a wash rag, put him to bed in his underwear, count what remained in his pants pockets, and cry the night away at the kitchen table.

The father got worse as the children grew. At lunch in the quarry, he was sullen and ate everything, leaving Bruno hungry. The nights at the tap-haus grew longer, and sometimes the father would come home after a beating and prove his toughness on his wife or children, especially young Bruno. Then he would cry and apologize.

"*I did not mind the beatings as much as the crying afterward,*" *Hauptmann said.* "*You can deal with a bastard if he's a bastard all the time. Worse is a bastard who makes you feel sorry for him.*"

The older children escaped as fast as they could. His sister ran away at sixteen to America with a middle-aged bachelor, a slightly hunch-backed Krementz shoemaker who wanted to leave behind the poverty of his hometown and the taunts of his neighbors.

"*They called him quasi-Quasimodo,*" *Hauptmann said.* "*I remember being so ashamed that my sister, no beauty herself,*" *nonetheless picked this creature to elope with to America. I was ten at the time, and my friends were merciless."*

A few years later his brothers, at sixteen and seventeen, enlisted together in the German Army and went off to fight in World War I.

"You know the American expression 'three hots and a cot'? That's why they went," Hauptmann said. "At least the army would feed them."

Bruno, thirteen, was left alone with his miserable parents. Both his brothers were injured in heavy artillery attacks in Alsace-Lorraine, but that didn't stop Bruno from escaping into the army.

"I was thrown in with hardened soldiers, grown men already weary of war and embittered by hardships," Hauptmann said. "I was shot at and gassed repeatedly as our army collapsed under pressure from you Americans. Many days, I thought I would die. Many nights, I asked God why he put me in such predicaments. Then I stopped believing there was a God, because a merciful God would never subject men made in his image to such horrors. I am right. This is a world without mercy or justice. It is a world where innocent boys are shot at and gassed for the supposed good of their country, a world where innocent men are electrocuted."

The world wouldn't get much better for young Hauptmann. He returned to Krementz after the armistice, convinced he was dying of consumption from nerve gas. His mother was starving. His father was found dead in a snow bank the winter before.

"There was not enough food in Germany. There were not enough clothes," Hauptmann said. "Here we were, Germans, living like primitive people in Sardinia or Africa or some other God-forsaken place."

With an Army friend named Fritz Petzold, Hauptmann went on a burglary spree. "Our first mark was Herr Schierach, the fat

Bürgermeister of Krementz. We did it for the effect and daring as much as the loot. We broke into his house while he dined with his fat wife at the only surviving restaurant in the village, and we found a stash of three hundred Marks and a silver watch we sold the next day in Dresden for another three hundred. Within a week, we found our second pigeon, a man named Eduard Scheumann who owned the leather tannery in town. We found two thousand Marks in his home, plus jewelry, which we sold in Dresden for another thousand. With the money I bought rich food—fruit, pate, and chocolates—and brought it home to my mother. It was like the old days with tea roots and berries, and my mother was so pleased. She asked me how I could afford it, and I said a bonus pension for men who had been gassed."

I told Hauptmann it was interesting how, in both cases, he and Fritz went after prominent people. They were modern-day Robin Hoods, I said, stealing from the fat and giving to the thin. I drew a parallel to the Lindbergh case.

"That is foolish," Hauptmann said with a dismissive wave. "I am not a stupid man. Far from it. Stealing from the mayor of a small German village may attract the attention of the local, incompetent constable. Stealing the baby of Charles Lindbergh would attract the attention of the world and every American law enforcement agency. Only an idiot would try that, and only an idiot would see similarities between the two cases. And, if you let me finish, you'll see we didn't only rob rich people."

To prove his point, Hauptmann told how he and Petzold mugged two women and stole their government food ration cards outside a market. Both women were young mothers pushing baby carriages. One was a war widow. The crime infuriated the people of Krementz, and police initiated a house-to-house search for clues.

"Yes, they were defenseless women but, as such, the government would have given them a new round of ration cards," Hauptmann said. "For men, it wasn't so easy."

The police found the victims' food cards at Petzold's house, and he promptly ratted out Hauptmann. Both were given five years of "three hots and a cot," but were paroled after two.

Hauptmann was thrown back in jail after a leather heist at Scheumann's tannery.

"I made new friends in prison. They were older, more organized criminals, men who knew how to exploit human greed and frailties; men who knew how to get things done."

These men helped him escape. A gate was left open and unattended by bribed guards one day for Hauptmann and a few others. Hauptmann made his way to Bremerhaven port, where he stowed away on the German liner Hanover. He was turned away at Ellis Island for lack of papers. Back in Germany, his friends had phony papers waiting for him. In the fall of 1923, he successfully entered the United States aboard a German luxury liner named, of all things, the SS George Washington.

"When I got to America, I had two cents in my pocket. Literally," he said.

"These people who helped you, did they force you to pay them back?" I asked, trying to wrangle the confession with empathy. "Is that why you kidnapped the baby?"

"Ridiculous, you and these theories," he said with another dismissive wave. "Do you not believe in the goodwill of men, even those who are criminals?"

"I don't believe in the goodwill of men, even those who aren't criminals," I said.

"I do not want to engage you in a philosophical discussion," he said. "I had enough of those in the German penitentiary."

For all Haines's previous admissions about how he had reduced humans to paper-thin characters for news stories, his back-and-forth with Bruno Hauptmann revealed a deeper understanding of human nature, a sensitivity that made him an adept interviewer. Later, when I complimented him on this, he described it as "guile."

"It's gaining trust for your own advantage," he said. "An unsavory character trait."

The manuscript went on to describe how Hauptmann found work as a carpenter and settled in the Bronx. A short time later he met Anna Schoeffler, a counter girl at a Danish bakery on Dyre Avenue. And at this point, Haines the interviewer stood out of the way and let Hauptmann begin his own emotional undoing. "It's another reporting trick, I call 'The Void of Silence,'" Haines said. "Keep your mouth shut and the other person will fill the uncomfortable void of silence. In the end, they'll tell you everything you want to know." So Haines let Hauptmann talk about his wife.

"You have seen my wife, she is no beauty," Hauptmann said. "I saw her many times before she caught my attention. But one day, as I sat drinking coffee, I was struck by her manner. She was polite but direct with customers and a very hard worker. While other girls would gossip about their boyfriends or flirt with customers, Anna worked—waiting on people, making coffee, arranging pastries. When there were no customers, she would wipe counters and glass cases with an ammonia rag, while the others did nothing but yak-yak-yak. There was a beautiful blonde waitress I went to see each day, but there was a goodness about Anna that overcame her plainness. I could tell she was a very decent woman, someone who was frugal and could help a man build his future. I forgot about the blonde beauty, who hadn't noticed me anyway, and began to think fondly of Anna.

"With my wife, it was not like some fairy tale. It was a slow, deliberate courtship. We were both lonely in America, but in no rush to fall for someone frivolous. I am not like that. I am too hardened a man. My wife, either. She is much too level-headed. She, too, had a hard life, both here and in Germany. Now, it's been made much worse ..."

He stopped and looked away, staring at the bars that separated him from the world outside, including Anna and little Bubi.

He was silent for a number of minutes—and I could tell he was deciding whether to unburden himself, maybe not of the crime, but of his deepest feelings. I stayed quiet for a moment then said, "Go ahead," in almost a whisper.

He looked back at me with tears in his eyes.

"My wife ... My wife is ..."

He then stopped again and composed himself. I shut up and let him talk.

"My wife and I got married and continued working hard. I was a carpenter and fix-it man, determined to stay out of trouble. There was no need. Unlike Germany, here work was plentiful. She stayed waitressing. Each night she came home and told me of rude and impatient people, and the men who made salacious comments to her. This infuriated me because she was a proper woman. My childhood left a bitter taste in my mouth. I was determined to never allow my wife and child to feel the shame and anger of poverty or ridicule."

I saw my opening to press him on a confession but let it pass, to let him build momentum and feel at ease with me.

He kept talking. With a partner from Germany, he dabbled in the fur business, and they invested their meager profits in stock. Hauptmann had only been in America a few years but he understood the game.

"In America, the man who gets richest isn't the man who designs the car or the man who builds the car. It's the man who supplies the gas," he said.

A year or so after the market crash, Hauptmann and his partner caught some rebounding stock and started making a little money. Hauptmann talked his wife into quitting the bakery, and soon after—and, coincidentally, not long after the ransom was delivered—he, too, was able to quit work and concentrate on investing.

"Why work with your hands when you can work with your head?" he said. "I could always build furniture or shelves as a hobby."

Of course, I already knew about Hauptmann's stock market charades. All this came out in court and, under cynical questioning by prosecutor Wilentz, Hauptmann had to admit he lost money in the market. Still, he did not return to work and had enough cash to buy a new car, new walnut furniture, and an expensive "stereophonic" radio in a fine-grained cabinet.

For the next two hours, I let him talk about his arrest and interrogation, the evidence against him and the evidence for him.

I empathized as he complained how he was bullied by the Jersey State Police, denied food and sleep for two days.

"They asked me the same questions a thousand different ways," he said.

I nodded in agreement as he complained about the jury ignoring his alibi witnesses.

"They believe the rich man, Lindbergh, when he says his butlers, maids, and nurses are honorable people who would never plot to kidnap a baby, but they don't believe my wife and friends—honest, working people—when they testify to my whereabouts on the night of the kidnapping. Why? Because we're German."

I didn't debate Hauptmann over these points. My strategy was to let him talk and not be adversarial, then bring the conversation back to his wife. Reilly, double-crossing bastard that he was, was right. It was the only way to uncover Hauptmann's true motivations, and therefore, uncover the truth about what happened the night the baby disappeared.

"Your wife," I said, "is a remarkably loyal woman. Some women won't stick with a man through a head cold, and your wife has stuck by your side and believed in your innocence through this whole ordeal. You're a lucky man."

"Lucky? You call this lucky?" he said with a snort. "I'm going to the electric chair, you fool!"

"Yes, but you're going to the electric chair knowing the woman you love loves you so much she can't fathom your guilt, despite all the evidence to the contrary."

"Please. You are not here to talk about my wife," he said, getting agitated.

"You'll die knowing this woman you love defended you till the end, alone in the face of overwhelming public opinion."

"Enough," he said and began to pace.

"You'll die knowing you are the most hated man in America, maybe even the world, and yet your plain and frail wife has shown immeasurable strength and courage by admitting her love for you by her actions."

"No more!" he yelled.

"That is a remarkable love, my friend. You say your love affair with Anna was not like some fairy tale. You're wrong! It is the most romantic love story I have ever heard. It is a legendary love. In my book, you are a lucky man to have known love like that. Not many men do."

Hauptmann stared at me blankly, blinked twice, then sat down abruptly and began to cry. I watched the muscles on his face contract as he winced to control his sobbing.

"Why do you do this to me?" he wailed. "Why do you ladle so much guilt on me?"

"I'm not trying to make you feel guilty, my friend. I'm trying to make you feel better," I said. "Men live with all kinds of emptiness, loneliness, and alienation. No man in the world is as alone as you are right now, yet few men are so loved by the woman they call their wife. Don't you see the grand irony?"

"What would you know about it?" Hauptmann snapped. "You, and all the others like you, newspapermen who make a living exploiting the troubles of others. What do you know of such things? You have no souls."

No soul? I wanted to say, Hey, pal, I'm not the one in here convicted of murdering a baby, but I instead kept my mouth shut.

Hauptmann kept on.

"Men like you, I know your type. I saw it during the war: writers who question the intelligence of leadership and the bravery of soldiers, all from the safety of some newspaper office in Bonn.

"Me, I have experienced real hardship. I am the man who has lived it, not watched it. You talk about loneliness and alienation. What do you know about these things? I have lived it, again and again and again."

His anger was building, so I let him keep talking.

"You say you are trying to make me feel better, telling me how lucky I am to have such a loving wife. You don't understand. You only think you understand. You make it sound like some fairy tale, some romantic drivel. Yes, she loves me! She loves me enough to be blind to the possibility of my guilt. But I love her, too. I love her enough to die for her. You, a man like you, can never understand this."

Hauptmann looked at me, not only in anger, but in that arrogant Aryan way the world has come to know and hate so well. He was challenging me, expecting an argument. I didn't give it to him.

Instead, I snuck up on him. I told him the story of Sara Lawson and how our love did not endure. I told him about my own son and his Down syndrome, a less-fortunate version of his innocent little Manfred, also orphaned from his father by circumstance. I told him about my own shame. Hauptmann listened intently, and I could tell he was somewhat surprised that I, interviewer and adversary, would share such intimate details of my life with him. It was my attempt to build trust. At the end of my story, I asked him why he thought Sara rejected me, a ploy to make him think I trusted him.

"Was it the repulsion she, like you, felt for my work, sordid as it must have seemed to her?" I asked. "Was it her fear of scandal and small-town whispers? Whatever it was, did her shame outweigh her feelings for me? How is it that your wife stands beside you, a convicted baby-killer, and my woman rejects me for simply printing a picture of the dead child? How does a man command such love?

"And me, why didn't I make one last stab at trying to win her? Why didn't I just wash my hands of this newspaper crud, give everything up to become a Hopewell yokel, and prove my love for her? What stopped me?"

Hauptmann thought for awhile.

"Because you are a coward," Hauptmann said. "You didn't know what sacrifice to make, so you did nothing. You didn't have the guts to make the right choice. So you ran and hid."

"Maybe you're right," I said with phony resignation, and let it sit for a second or two. "Or maybe I knew what sacrifice to make. I sacrificed her. I freed her to go on with her life. Maybe

I sacrificed my happiness to let her go on her own way. That's heroic, isn't it?"

"Maybe," Hauptmann said. "But maybe you imprisoned her, did you ever think of that? If she loved you as much as you claim—which I doubt, but for the sake of discussion, let's say she did—you condemned her to life without you. You are a coward. And she is a coward, too. She did not stand by you, like my Anna stands by me. Your girl ran at the first hint of trouble. My Anna ... she does not run. She stays by my side, no matter what it is I've done."

And at that moment, I knew I had him, the haughty son of a bitch!

"You say I've condemned my girl to life without me," I said. "Aren't you doing the same thing to your poor wife? Aren't you, too, a coward, condemning Anna to life without you? If you confessed, the state would spare your life, such as it is, and you could at least see your wife and baby once a month on visitation days."

"You're a fool! Such a fool!" he shouted, again up out of his seat. "This scenario you paint is ridiculous. If I confess, I condemn her to a worse fate! She must live with the knowledge and shame that her husband—the man she loved and stood by faithfully—killed that baby, a baby no different than our little Bubi. She will know that I lied and deceived her from the start. It will be a pain much deeper than my death.

"I'm not a stupid man, Mr. Haines. Far from it. From the minute the police arrested me, I knew what sacrifice I had to make to protect my Anna. I am prepared to die for her!"

"So you did it."

"Your justice system says I did. And, as you said yourself, that is all that counts in America."

"No, sir," I said. "Your justice system, the one that resides in your gut, says you did. You did it, and you can't confess because it would shame your wife. So you'd rather die than hurt her."

Hauptmann said nothing.

"So instead, you'll condemn her to a life of defending you," I said. "Defending the lie of your innocence."

"At least I won't be around to see it," he said. "The one way, I have to live with my guilt and what my guilt will do to her. The other way, I condemn her to a life connected to me, a baby-killer. Some choice I have, eh?"

Hauptmann hung his head and began to cry.

"Better she lives a lie, than she lives the truth," he said.

Then he stopped abruptly.

"That's all I will tell you," he said and straightened his face and his back. "Except that it was never intended for the baby to die. That was a horrible accident. Now I want this over. I want it to end for me, and my Anna. Let her think the state put to death an innocent man. It will give her more peace than if she knows I'm guilty."

"And what about Mrs. Lindbergh? Does she deserve any peace?" I asked.

"She has her husband to share her grief. My wife will be alone."

He wiped away his tears, washing away the softness that had overcome him. His stubbornness set back in, like concrete hardening in fast motion.

"I will never make an official confession. Never. I will never reveal the details that pin me to the crime. Never. I will die with my secret. That is all I have to say to you and your lousy newspaper, Mr. Haines. You said you wanted my story, but what you really wanted was my confession. You cannot have it."

"But I do have it."

"Yes, but not in a tangible way," he said. "You have my vague admission, yes, but no precious details to support it. You know I did it, but you have no facts. Those I will take to my grave. If you write I confessed, I will deny it. And then we'll see who your America believes—a criminal or a rag-sheet reporter!"

"I guess we'll see," I said and stood to pack up my things.

And that's when Hauptmann sprang on me. He grabbed the lapels of my coat, but instead of roughing me up, he sank. He was clinging to me.

"If you have a decent bone in your body, if you have an ounce of compassion in your blood, please do not put this in your newspaper. It would kill my wife and shame my son. Better they go through life thinking I might be innocent, rather than knowing I am guilty. I'm asking you, man-to-man, as a dying wish for my family, show me mercy. Show me mercy you know I don't deserve."

I pulled him up, then called for the guard.

"I told him nothing!" Hauptmann yelled as I was led out. "I told him nothing."

Back at the hotel, the phone was ringing.

It was Dicks.

"Did he confess?"

"Look, I got everything from his boyhood in Germany right up to his conviction in New Jersey. The whole story," I said.

"Look, Haines, nobody wants that," Dicks said. "Did he confess?"

I didn't know what to say. I was still thinking it through. On one side, the glory of the byline and Hearst's cash bonus; on the other, poor Anna Hauptmann and her half-orphaned son. The glory would be gone in a day, the cash in a year, but the public humiliation and contempt for the Hauptmanns would be forever.

Hauptmann was right; if she believed in his innocence, she could hold her head high. Who was I to steal that?

"Haines? Haines! Did he confess?"

Then I thought of Sara and my little boy, spared a lesser humiliation, but humiliation just the same, of being the bastard son of a man like me, a man capable of publishing a dead baby's photo. We were accomplices, me and Hauptmann. The case he created, and the way I covered it, hurt the women we loved so very badly. Anna and Sara, residual victims of the Lindbergh baby kidnapping. I thought of Mrs. Lindbergh, and I felt a congestive sadness spread through my chest.

"Haines, goddamn you! What's going on? Did he confess?"

For many years after, I tried to understand what I did next.

Maybe I decided to keep Bruno's secret so my own secret would have company in my private darkness.

Or maybe I was, once-and-for-all, just tired of making a name off other people's misery.

"Listen, Haines, I'm not in the mood. I got the entire Hearst organization breathing down my neck, plus I got a bonus riding on this, just like you. What happened in there?"

Or maybe I was just sick of being pushed around by Dicks.

"Haines, you son-of-a-bitch. I want a big headline that says, BRUNO: I DID IT. Now for the last time, goddamn you, did he confess?"

I thought of Hauptmann's last words to me. "If you have a decent bone in your body, if you have an ounce of compassion in your blood ..."

"No, Dicks. I'm telling you the truth. He didn't. He stuck to his story, same as always."

Epilogue

The manuscript ended there. The next morning, back at the Oceanview, over powdered eggs and oatmeal, I asked Haines why he never tried to publish it.

"Arthritis, mostly," he said and held up his curved, stiff fingers. "It needed too much work. That, and when I moved in here, the clacking of the typewriter was so loud and lonely I lost my nerve for it."

"So what happened after?"

"Nothing is what happened," Haines said. "Dicks cursed me out. He screamed, 'Winchell always said you were a lousy reporter and a worse writer and he was right!'

"I gave it right back to him, though. 'Then why didn't you send Winchell in?' I'll tell you why, because Winchell didn't have the guts or the guile. Because they knew it was a losing proposition from the start, and they didn't want the mighty Winchell to fail."

"None of it ever ran?"

"I typed up my notes, stopping short of Hauptmann's admission, and Dicks gave them to a rewrite guy. They ran an 'exclusive interview' but Dicks was right—nobody cared about the human side of Richard Hauptmann. They wanted the evil Bruno. They wanted the confession, but I kept it to myself."

Haines did some mop-up work for the *Mirror*, covering the appeals and legal machinations over the next year.

"Then I was pretty much off the story, but a few days before the execution, Dicks called. 'I want you in Trenton for Hauptmann's execution,' he said.

"'No, thanks,' I said. 'I don't have the stomach to cover this one.'

"'Who said anything about covering? Winchell's going to write,' Dicks said. 'I want you to sneak in the ankle camera, like Ruth Snyder.'

"'Forget it, Dicks,' I said. 'I've done enough tangling with Jersey state cops. I'll get arrested.'

"'C'mon, Haines,' Dick pleaded. 'It was your brilliant idea back with Mrs. Snyder. You can pull it off.'

"'Tell you what,' I said. 'I'll get the ankle camera and teach Winchell how to work it.'

"Of course, Dicks didn't go for that. He said, 'If Winchell gets caught and thrown in jail, who's going to write the story?'

"That's when I hung up on him."

When Bruno Hauptmann was executed on April 3, 1936, Fred Haines spent the night on his front porch, bundled up in a sweater and a couple of blankets, smoking cigarettes and drinking scotch, watching bay waves lap the shore.

"I refused to go, and that was that," Haines said.

"Did they fire you?"

"Fire me? Hell, no! I was sour on the business, but I still went in most places head first. Dicks knew that. I was a tabloid guy. I quit soon enough, but on my terms."

***

Haines's last day as a newspaperman began on Halloween Eve in 1938.

"I was on my porch with a drink, watching the harvest moon climb over the ocean, until I went to bed. At 3 AM, again like with the Morro Castle, my phone rang. It was Dicks."

"'Tell me this is a nightmare,' I said.

"He said, 'Believe me, this is no joke. Some radio actor named Orson Welles did a show called "The War of the Worlds." He made it sound like a news broadcast, and a few idiots think the Martians landed. Old Man Hearst wants the story to make radio look bad, dangerous even. He wants a story that says it caused a mass panic down in Jersey where these Martians supposedly landed.'

"This was the War of the Worlds, all right," Haines said. "But it wasn't Martians versus Earthlings—it was Radio invading Newspaper Land! See, in those days, everybody was predicting radio would put us out of business. Radio could deliver news faster, and you could hear the authentic voices of people in the news, like FDR in his fireside chats. Lots of people thought radio would be the end of newspapers. Same thing happened when TV came along and will happen again when the next gadget comes along."

He was right, of course. He said this in 1999, before the internet really took off. Like the mediums before it, the internet delivers news faster and more efficiently than the paper. But the very nature of such speed appeals to short attention spans. Good journalism appeals to the readers left among us. Good newspaper people know that. Bad newspaper people still think they're in the news delivery business, rather than in the journalism business. So what's the first thing they throw overboard when their paper is struggling? Journalists. Fewer reporters equal less news. Less news equals fewer reasons to read. They shrink the paper to save the cost of news print. A smaller paper carries less news. They divest in their own product. They undermine their reason for being; they shrink their relevance. That's why they're doomed.

The heart of the story was in Grover's Mill, a farm village outside Princeton where the Martians crash-landed and came out throwing fireballs. Overnight news reports said some frightened locals had packed up and fled, while others grabbed their shotguns and started blasting at shadows.

"We New York tabloid guys made them all out to be gullible country rubes and fools, and the *Mirror* afternoon edition ran a picture of an old, rubber-faced guy pointing a shotgun toward the sky," Haines said. "You know what else? It was the first case I ever recall of media covering media. Newspapers everywhere whined about the blurred line between radio news and entertainment, while radio blared about its power to spontaneously reach the masses. Hello, advertisers! Everybody was hyperventilating, puffing up on their own self-importance. Heywood Broun wrote in the *World-Telegram* that government should outlaw such dramatic broadcasts. Dorothy Thompson of the *Post* said radio left us open to 'the persuasive propaganda and theatrical demagoguery of the Third Reich.' Hah! And they said *I* couldn't write!"

Haines got to Grover's Mill in the morning.

"It was like my trip to Hopewell, except in daylight. Same country roads to nowhere," he said. "Twice I stopped to pee in the woods."

The town was little more than a collection of 19th-century wood houses next to a mill pond in the center of a farm belt. Haines found the feed store, where a group of men in jeans and flannel shirts drank coffee by the loading dock. Some had come in pickup trucks, others by horse-drawn wagons.

"One old farmer told me they weren't fooled because the make-believe Martians landed on a make-believe farm," Haines said.

"'They said the *Wilmuth* farm on the radio,' the old guy said, 'but I've been here my whole life and nobody around here's named Wilmuth, and nobody around here ever heard of any Wilmuth farm. I knew it was baloney.'

"The interview with 'Farmer Wilmuth' was even more bogus," Haines scoffed.

"'The guy on the radio was trying to sound like a hick,' another farmer said. 'He sounded like some Mississippi hayseed. Do we sound like that to you? It was the phoniest thing I ever heard. Anybody listening should have known right then that the whole thing was a joke.'"

Haines stayed in town for awhile to interview more people. Everywhere he got the same story: Anybody who was fooled had to *be* a fool.

"Just before I left, I stopped back at the feed store. The *Mirror* had come in, and the same men were looking at the front page picture of the rubber-faced guy.

"'Wait'll old Byram sees this,' one of them said. 'When he does, there'll be hell to pay!'

"Just then a dented Model A pickup pulled into the lot, kicking up dust. It was the guy with the rubber face.

"'Oooh, boy,' said one of the old farmers."

Old Byram got out of his truck and headed straight for Haines.

"The only guys in town in suits that day were reporters, so he made me pretty quick.

"'You one of these New York rag sheet writers?' he asked.

"'Frederick G. Haines, *New York Daily Mirror*,' I said, and as soon as the 'M' got out of mouth I knew I'd made a mistake."

Old Byram did an about-face back to his truck, reached in, and came out with a single-barrel shotgun. He pumped it and headed back for Haines.

"Next thing, he starts reciting, '*Mirror, mirror on the wall, what paper tells the biggest fibs of all?*'

"I was trying to tough it out, figuring the old coot was just trying to scare me. Then he said, 'Well, lookie here, boys ... well, I'll be—it's one of them there Martian critters. Get on outta here before I blast ye, ye spaceman varmint!'

"The other men all laughed and I tried to laugh along, but I could feel my smile was weak. It got weaker when old Byram brought the gun up to my eye level.

"'You New York newspaper fellas made me look like a goddam bumpkin,' he said. 'You want a bumpkin, I'll give you a bumpkin. I'll show you who's shootin' Martians!'"

The other men stopped laughing when old Byram pumped the gun again.

"'Uhhh, Mister, I think he's serious,' one of them said to Haines. 'If I were you, I'd get up outta here.'"

Haines put his hands up in surrender, but the coot snapped back the trigger.

"Right then I knew he was more than serious, he was *intent*," Haines said. "I turned tail, but hadn't taken more than two steps when I heard a blast and felt a razor-strap burn in my backside. I jumped, and the men busted out laughing.

"'I've been shot,' I screamed, grabbing my behind and the shredded seat of my pants. 'I've been shot!'"

The laughter grew even more raucous.

"'You haven't been shot, son,' one of the farmers managed to say. 'You've been peppered with rock salt. That's what we do around here to keep dogs away from our sheep.'"

Haines smiled at me as he slowly stirred some brown sugar into his oatmeal.

"Keeping dogs from sheep. That pretty much summed it up." He laughed. "I decided right then and there I was going to stop running with the pack. I called Dicks from the nearest pay phone and quit. He didn't try to stop me."

"Did you ever regret it?" I asked.

"Nope. It was the perfect ending, a final irony. After all the lies and paper-thin heroes and villains and victims I made up, I was shot by a guy who was ticked at being portrayed as something he was not, over a story that never happened. None of it was real, except the shot in my ass!"

***

Frederick G. Haines disappeared, and Fred Haines found work as a flack for Bell Laboratories, staying there through the 1960s.

"With war coming, I was glad to be out of the newspaper business—away from the overwhelming sadness and despair the world was about to experience again. I'd had my fill of tragedies and heartaches, what we call the news.

"After the war, during the Cold War years, Bell Labs was exciting in its own way," he said. "They invented the transistor and the computer chip and other important stuff, and I wrote up the press releases. Here I was, an old newspaperman writing about the Information Age. What a hoot!"

He joined a local ambulance squad and spent his spare time either at the first aid shack or on the porch of his home in the Highlands, watching the world sail or fly by. In the early '70s he began "Bruno's Confession." He worked on it with little urgency until he moved to the Oceanview, then stopped completely.

"I never intended to publish the story of what happened in Hauptmann's cell," he said. "There were a few times—one was around the 25th anniversary of the crime—I considered it, but just as Anna Hauptmann's grace prevented her husband from confessing, her grace also kept me from revealing it. I felt the same way at the 50th anniversary."

Back in February of 1935, Hauptmann told Haines his confession would condemn his wife to a lifetime of shame. But by not confessing, he condemned her to a lifetime of trying to prove his innocence, just as Haines had predicted. She died in 1994 on what would have been their 69th wedding anniversary. She was 95 and spent her last pennies to hire some scheister lawyer to open up the FBI files on the case. There was nothing in them to prove he was innocent, just guilty as ever. From time to time, Haines read about her attempts to clear her husband's name. Each time, it reduced his conflict over holding the story.

"I never met Anna Hauptmann," he told me. "And the last time I saw her was the day the verdict was announced in Flemington. But I admired how she didn't play to the cheap seats with the nation watching—her sobs were not theatrical, but suppressed and dignified. And in all the years since, I admired her for her stubborn, maybe even dumb, belief in his innocence against all logic, and her unconditional love of his memory against all odds. I had no right to puncture that innocence or damage that love."

Haines said he started the manuscript for only one reason: to keep it all straight in his head.

"When Hauptmann was executed, I never had to worry about him confessing to some other newsman. But now the story was all mine. Like when Sara died, our story was all mine. I wanted to make sure I kept it right, even if I was never going to share it."

"So why share it now? And why with me?" I asked him.

He paused to gather his thoughts. "Good question. It's one I've thought about since you walked in the door.

"I guess, now, because everybody is dead but me. It's a part of history. True history. Somebody should know it. And you, because you're the fella who happened to come by. You got the random assignment, sort of like me the night the baby was kidnapped. You got it. And you get it! You're a smart guy and I like you, so I'm telling you because I had to tell somebody. Might as well be you."

"Thank you," I said and reached over to pat his arm. He intercepted my hand with his and gave it a powerful squeeze.

"No—thank *you*," he said. "Look, I'm an old man, alone in the world. Bruno Hauptmann told me his story from his jail cell in a courthouse cellar. I'm telling it to you from my own prison, in the place I've come to die. He told me, knowing he was going to the electric chair. Me, I'm counting down my days, and I don't want the story to die with me. So you have it now—it's yours. All of it. Do what you want with it."

"What do *you* want me to do with it?" I asked.

Haines shook his head at the stupidity of the question.

"I told you, didn't I?"

***

I visited Fred Haines regularly until his death, every Wednesday afternoon and most Sundays. On nice days, I would wheel him down the boardwalk in Ocean Grove, and the sea air would revitalize him. The stories kept coming, some about his newspaper days and all the truth-bending he did, but mostly about his first aid work and hurricanes and floods along the Jersey shore.

One day, as we were sitting in the Oceanview solarium, he said, "Give me a minute to feel sorry for myself. There's a lesson in it for you.

"Look at me, stuck inside a place like this, watching the world go by. I have spent so much of my life on the outside looking in. It's a pitfall of being a newspaperman, I guess. You're a critic, not a creator, like you said. You cover, you don't participate. It's safer that way. It saved us from being responsible for our own lives, just like you said. For the best years of my life, really, I handed my life over to the newspaper and the story *du jour*. There was always something new to giddyap on, to run yourself to exhaustion over, then recover on a bar stool, then start all over again the next day. It was always go, go, go. Let me tell you—warn you, I really mean—it hollows you out. Nothing felt worthwhile until I quit watching and put myself on the handle ends of the stretcher."

His tone began to gain altitude, lifting from sad resignation to something closer to angry regret.

"So much of my life was like looking at a museum diorama. Ruth Snyder, the Lindberghs, whatever. I looked at a scene, then described it. I never lived it. When Sara came into my life, she took my hand and tried to show me the possibilities of creating—and living—my own scenes. She was saying, 'Here, Freddy, here's what you can have. A wife, children. A tidy house and a cozy existence. Just stop looking from the outside, and come in. Come in. Come in and lead a normal life.'

"But I ran back out, to the observer's side of the glass, because that's where I was most comfortable. That's what I knew. New day, new story, turn the page. It wasn't until that moment in Hauptmann's cell that I knew how to be a participant. I made news. And I did the right thing with it. Same thing with the *Hindenburg*. I didn't just cover it. I lived it.

"Someday, if you stay in this business long enough, you'll realize what you missed by covering everything," he said. "Are you listening to me?"

I was. His regrets about being a critic rather than a creator stuck with me. I had sensed it was happening to me, too, but when he threw my own words back at me, they solidified. It was a rock through my window and will shape the rest of my life. Some changes have to be made, and if I give myself half a chance, maybe I'll find a Sara of my own—and hang on to her.

Fred Haines was my last newspaper story. The first part ran the last weekend of December 1999, on the eve of a new millennium. The headline was WITNESS TO HISTORY: *OCEANVIEW RESIDENT COVERED BIG NEWS OF THE CENTURY*. Trust me, the story itself was nearly as flat and bland as the headline. I reduced Haines to paper-thinness. His true story, the one you've read here, could not be contained in a few columns of newsprint, so I left out all about his beautiful Sara and Bruno's confession. Besides, Haines was still alive.

"The right time will be after," he agreed.

I promised him I would write it like he told it.

He died in his sleep in the spring of 2005. The Oceanview called me, as he had instructed, and I got there in time to sit alone with his body for a little while before the morticians came. He was at peace, his face relaxed into the slightest smile. Somewhere out there, in our infinite universe of unknown dimensions, I hoped the particles of his soul had reunited with the parts of Sara's he loved so much. The spirits of Freddy and Sara, from their time and space, intertwined and dancing into eternity. That's how I like to imagine it.

I wrote his obituary, filed it, then quit the paper to write this book. I gave his eulogy in the same solarium at the Oceanview where I first met him, in front of all the ladies who loved his stories.

In the end, I was the closest thing to family Fred Haines had.

Sad?

Maybe.

But he left this story, which now belongs to all of us.

About the Author

Mark Di Ionno is a columnist at *The Star-Ledger*, New Jersey's largest newspaper. He is four-time winner of the New Jersey Press Association's first-place award for column writing.

Di Ionno got his start in newspapers as a Navy journalist and has been a reporter, editor, and columnist his entire adult life. Prior to writing for *The Star-Ledger*, he was a sports columnist at the *New York Post*.

He is an adjunct professor of journalism at Rutgers–Newark, his alma mater, and has written three award-winning books on New Jersey history and culture.

The Last Newspaperman is his first novel.